LONG CLIMB TO THE TOP

LONG CLIMB TO THE TOP

PARKS PAT MYSTERIES #2

P.D. WORKMAN

Copyright © 2021 by P.D. Workman

ISBN: 9781774680674 (IS Hardcover)

ISBN: 9781774680667 (IS Paperback)

ISBN: 9781774680681 (IS Large Print)

ISBN: 9781774680636 (KDP Paperback)

ISBN: 9781774680643 (Kindle)

ISBN: 9781774680650 (ePub)

pdworkman

AND MORE AT PDWORKMAN.COM

.

*To those who are
leaving legacies*

STYLE NOTE

Since my largest readership is in the USA, I have chosen to use US spellings throughout this series. That includes the Americanization of centre to center, even where it is an actual place name, just for consistency's sake. I apologize to my Canadian readers for this.

I have chosen, however, to use Canadian grammar, particularly for Canadian voices. If you see what you think is a grammar error, it may just be Canadian, eh?

CHAPTER ONE

Margie Patenaude didn't need to be a detective to know who had left the dirty dishes in the sink.

"Christina!"

"Gotta go, Mom," Christina said, rushing into the room. She swept her long black hair out of the way as she shouldered her backpack so that it would not get caught under the strap. "The bus will be here any second. I'll see you after school." She headed toward the front door. "Oh, and you remember what I told you, right, about the Métis Club meeting after school today? So I'll be late. Don't expect me right after school."

"You left dishes in the sink—"

"I have to go. If I stop and do them now, I'll miss the bus, and then you'll need to drive me to school." Christina had the door open and was halfway out. "Sorry. I'll load the dishwasher tonight. Okay? Bye!"

Margie watched her fifteen-year-old race across the street to the bus stop. And she was right, of course; the bus was making its way down the street, and if she had taken an extra ten seconds to have a conversation or rinse off the dishes, she would have missed it. But that was no excuse for Christina to leave them in the sink in the first place, when she knew she was supposed to rinse them and put them directly into the dishwasher.

She sighed and did it herself. She had to drive into work, and the other homicide detectives and Sergeant MacDonald wouldn't know whether she had left five minutes later because of her daughter or if she had just hit the lights wrong or run into a traffic snarl on Blackfoot Trail. She checked the table and counter for any other orphaned dishes and didn't find any. In another minute, she had the dishwasher running, Stella was settled for the day, and Margie was walking at a quick clip out to her car. It was a cool, crisp morning.

"Oh, Detective Pat!" called Mrs. Rose, a sweet little old lady who was the first and only owner of the 1960s bungalow next to Margie's.

Margie stopped, anxious to get on her way but not willing to be rude or pretend that she hadn't heard Mrs. Rose's call. She took a couple of steps toward her neighbor, but stopped the prescribed two meters away. "Yes, Mrs. Rose? What can I do for you?"

"I just wanted to make sure that you had heard that the 55+ Society is open again."

Margie's expression must have betrayed her consternation at this announcement. Mrs. Rose smiled her sweet, pink-lipstick smile. "The 55+ Society. It's over there on Twenty-Sixth Avenue, where your grandfather lives."

"Oh, yes...?"

"And it's been closed since the whole pandemic thing. But they've opened up again. And they have lots of programs for the seniors in the area. You should take a look at the activities and clubs that they run, see if there is anything that your grandfather would like to go to."

"Oh! Okay, I will," Margie agreed. She would see if there were anything that might interest Moushoom. "Thank you for letting me know."

"They probably have flyers in the lobby of the building he lives in. But if they don't, the 55+ Society is just about a block away.

You can stop in there any time they are open and get their program guide. And they can give you a tour. They're very helpful over there."

"That's great. I'm glad you let me know." Margie gave Mrs. Rose a firm nod, then turned back toward her car. "Have a wonderful day."

"I will, dear. You too."

❧

THE WORKDAY PASSED QUICKLY. The homicide team was working on a number of open cases, but none of them was burning hot. It was a matter of chasing down leads one at a time. Doing background checks on persons of interest, interviewing them, looking for connections or alibis. The day-to-day work of a homicide department.

She found it easier to move from one case to another than to stay focused on one all day, so she gathered shorter tasks from the primary investigator on each of the cases, read the file to bring herself up to speed, and worked on her assignment. Then she would jump to the next case.

No one on the team seemed to mind her ADHD approach. They were happy to have some of the less-desirable tasks taken off of their hands. Margie was eyeing the clock, trying to decide whether she would have time to review one more case before leaving for the day when Sergeant MacDonald—Mac—walked up to her desk. He was a tall man, towering over her when she was sitting down. His hair was almost entirely silver and he had lines of 'experience' around his mouth. He readjusted his thin-rimmed glasses.

"Yes, sir?" Margie immediately tried to think of what she might have done to attract his attention. Good or bad, she didn't want to be under the sergeant's scrutiny too often. Too much praise from him and the rest of the team would resent her, and too much criticism… well, any criticism was likely to keep Margie up

3

half the night with anxiety over her mistake and how to avoid making it again in the future. No one liked being criticized, and Margie felt that she was particularly thin-skinned about it. She criticized herself for not accepting criticism well. How was that for a fault?

"I've got a case for you. I know you like to be home when your daughter gets home from school, but this one is going to need your immediate attention."

The duty room was still as everyone else listened in. Margie had just solved the Fish Creek Park murder case. The next case should have gone to someone else. Although everyone else already had active files and Margie did not, so maybe that was why he had picked her.

"Uh, yes sir. She's going to be later today and, of course, when it's urgent, I can take the time I need to get started on it. She's old enough to be on her own for a few hours if I'm needed elsewhere."

She didn't ask him what he had for her but, of course, that was the question on the minds of everyone in the room.

Mac nodded his appreciation. He ran his fingers through his short gray hair and leaned on her desk. "Here's the thing. It's the same MO as the Fish Creek Park murder."

Margie's eyes went wide. She stared at him in surprise. "The same MO?"

Robinson had been killed with a single stab wound. Margie had caught the killer. So they knew that it wasn't the same killer. Just because another person was killed by a stab wound, that didn't make it the same killer or the same case.

"The same MO," MacDonald agreed. "It's another provincial park. Male victim. Single stab wound with a single-edged blade. Bled out. No apparent provocation, no one heard yelling or was aware that anything was wrong. Body discovered by a family walking the trail with a toddler in a stroller."

Not a dog-walker this time. But Margie was sure there were probably a number of dog-walkers close by. That one difference didn't make the case different from the Fish Creek murder.

She hoped that the toddler hadn't seen anything and wasn't old enough to remember it later. Hopefully, she had been sleeping peacefully in the stroller at the time. It was a good time for an afternoon nap.

"Okay. I'll look up this park and go see," Margie agreed. "Is it near Fish Creek Park?"

"No. Halfway to Cochrane. It's actually outside of Calgary city limits, but we are heading it up because of the connection to the Fish Creek case. Since it looks like the same killer."

"It's not, though," Margie pointed out.

"There's always the possibility that we got the wrong person for the Fish Creek murder."

"But he admitted to it. We didn't get the wrong person."

"I don't think so either. But innocent people do confess. It's also possible that he was released on bail or under his foster father's supervision and is no longer in custody."

"But if this other park isn't close to his home... how would he get there? He couldn't walk there like he did to Fish Creek. Is there a bus that goes all the way out there?"

"No, I don't think there's any bus service out there. Tours maybe. I'm sure it's not related. But because of the similarity in the cases and the sites of the homicide, it's your case."

"Okay. Give me the details." Margie looked at her watch. If she remembered correctly, Cochrane was west, toward the mountains. Margie's home was in the east, on the opposite side of the city. She was going to be more than an hour or two late getting home for Christina. Just the travel time would add an extra hour, forget any investigative work and waiting for someone from the medical examiner's office.

"Glenbow Ranch Provincial Park," Sergeant MacDonald told her. He spelled it out for her. "Do you want directions?"

"Will it be on my GPS? If it's outside of the city, it might not be..."

"Should be. It opened in 2011, so it's been there long enough".

CHAPTER TWO

Margie hit the road, driving west down Crowchild Trail. Rush hour appeared to have already hit and both Memorial Drive and Crowchild Trail were heavy with traffic. Progress was slow, which meant she would be all that much later getting home to Christina. She couldn't rush things at the murder scene. It would take time to process the scene. That was just the way it was. She used her Bluetooth to send a message to Christina, giving her an update and asking her to let Margie know when she was home.

There were several C-Train stations down the middle of Crowchild, and the trains ran past her every few minutes. They were packed with people. Despite the pandemic and all of the new protocols to follow, a lot of people were back to working downtown, and they all needed to get home to the outlying areas. She glanced as another train went by. Most people were masked, in compliance with the by-law recently put into place mandating masks in public places and the transit system in particular. Infection numbers were down, and she hoped that they stayed low despite the reopening of the schools.

Over to her right, there was a big white temple spire with a gold figure on top. The speed of the traffic was picking up, so she couldn't gawk at it for long, but it was pretty. A surprise to see something like that at the edge of the city. In another minute, she had reached city limits and Crowchild Trail had turned into Highway 1A.

There were rolling hills, but not a lot of trees like she had expected to see. She remembered how thickly Fish Creek Park had been treed and had expected the same type of scenery. There were fields and farmyards and small stands of trees here and there.

After a while, the GPS warned her to get into the left lane, and Margie obeyed, though she couldn't see any sign of the park. It seemed strange to have a park all the way out there. They wouldn't get foot traffic like Fish Creek Park did. A road sign announced that Glenbow Park was three kilometers away, but the GPS urged her to turn immediately. She watched for a break in the oncoming traffic and turned left onto a gravel road. Once on the gravel road, there were a few houses off to the left and thick trees to the right. The gravel road was on an incline, down into a valley. Margie slowed down and took the gravel and the curves in the road carefully.

Zipping down them like it was an emergency wouldn't do her any good. She couldn't save the man who was already dead, and if she ended up with her car in the ditch, it was just going to take that much longer to get done. Not to mention the reputation she would get. Detectives often ended up with nicknames within the department, and she did not want to be "Ditch" Patenaude.

It was farther than she would have expected. There was a public parking area, but Margie saw a gray-shirted officer standing up by a locked gate, watching the incoming traffic. She drove up to him. He bent down to talk through her window. He wasn't wearing a mask, and Margie pulled back, a little irritated that he would get so close to her.

"Are you the detective?" he asked. "Uh, Detective Pat?"

"Patenaude," Margie agreed. "That's me."

"Come on through, and drive down to the parking area beside

the house." He pointed in the direction of a big ranch house. "I'll walk down to you after I lock up here."

Margie waited while he swung the big gate open, then drove down to the lot he had pointed to. The house had perhaps been someone's home before the creation of the park. It had the feel of a family home rather than a conference or education center built by the government.

Margie put on her mask and got out and stretched, looking around. After the golden brown grass on the fields and hills up above, she had expected a stark setting. But down in the valley, there was lush green growth—lots of trees, long grass, and wild-flowers. Bees buzzed around her and orange butterflies fluttered here and there. Despite being the site of a murder, everything seemed peaceful and pleasant.

The Conservation Officer who had let her in the gate walked down to her. "Is this your first time in the park?"

"Yes. I'm just new to Calgary. So I've seen Fish Creek Park, but that's about it. I guess you heard about that."

"Yeah. It was in the news and as soon as we came across the body here... well, it was just too similar to ignore. We called the RCMP; it's their jurisdiction, but they looped your department in right away. You're the one with the deep knowledge on the Fish Creek case, so you get control."

"Is the RCMP already here?"

"They sent a couple of guys out. Our Conservation Officers controlled the scene. Just waiting on you."

"How about the forensic team and the medical examiner? Have they been notified?"

"Notified, but not here yet. It takes a while to get out here, as I'm sure you found." He looked at his watch. "An hour since we called you. And it's rush hour."

Margie nodded. "Okay, thanks. So, where is your body? I gather it's not in the house?" She tilted her head toward it.

"No. We all manage to get along pretty well in the Park Office." He gave her a roguish grin. "No murders there yet."

Margie smiled.

"I'm CO Richardson." He put out his hand to shake.

Margie shook her head. "Sorry, no unnecessary contact," she apologized. He should have known that. The police force, by the nature of their contact with the public at large, were already at higher risk of infection. She didn't want to be out of work due to a virus or quarantine, or to inadvertently pass something on to Moushoom, who was vulnerable due to his age.

Richardson rolled his eyes and lowered his hand. "If you'll come with me, I will take you to the scene."

Margie nodded. She got out of the car. "How far is it? I can walk a ways…"

At Fish Creek Park, the murder site had been too far from the parking lot for her to comfortably walk there to investigate. She hoped that the distance would be shorter at Glenbow.

"We have almost forty kilometers of trails. The body is only a couple of clicks away, but if you want to get home to your family tonight…" He looked at his watch. Margie was sure he wanted to get back to his regular duties as well, or to sign off at the end of his day. A murder scene might be an exciting novelty, but preserving the scene and dealing with curious visitors would be a pain. And it got dark early this late in the year. Everyone would want to have the scene cleared before it was too dark to see.

"Lead the way," Margie sighed. "One of these days, I'm going to have to come explore some of these parks for recreation instead of a murder investigation."

"You like to walk?"

"Yes, I do. I'd like to do more. There are some multi-use trails near my house, but so far, all I've been able to do is walk the dog on the closest ones."

"Where do you live?"

"In the southeast." Margie knew enough now not to mention that it was close to Forest Lawn or part of Greater Forest Lawn. She didn't think that the area warranted the reputation it seemed to have all over the city. "Near Pearce Estate Park, if you know where that one is?"

"Oh, sure. Harvie Passage is over there. Where the weir used to be."

Margie shrugged, not sure of any of this. Richardson correctly interpreted her reaction.

"The weir was there for a lot of years. People would go boating or fishing over there, or swim or fall in, and they would get killed in the weir, because of the way that the water going over the weir would create a circular flow." He twirled a finger horizontally to demonstrate. "Getting caught in it would just keep spinning you over and over, like being stuck in a washing machine."

"Oh."

"So eventually, they built out a series of rapids to replace the weir. They take rafters down the river in a series of steps so it is not so dangerous. It took a few tries to get it right, but it's all in place now, much better than it was. It's named the Harvie Passage, after the same family as used to live here," he pointed to the ranch house as he led her to the garage, "the same family as donated the lands for the park."

"Wow. A pretty philanthropic family."

"They are," he agreed. "There are a lot of things named after them and after Glenbow in and around Calgary. You'll come across a lot of them. The Glenbow Museum. The Dorothy Harvie Gardens. The Glenbow Park Ranch Foundation was set up by the family and shares this building with Alberta Parks. The foundation runs the Visitor Center, other park education and programming, and various other projects."

He used a keypad to let himself into the garage and directed Margie to one of the golf carts waiting there. "We'll drive over in this."

In a few minutes, they were driving slowly down the pathway, working their way past the walkers, runners, and cyclists enjoying an afternoon at the park. It was a more open area with little shade, and she could see the rolling vistas. She could see mountains on the horizon, under bright blue sky and washboard clouds. She turned her head to look back toward the city. She could see the downtown skyline in the other direction.

"Do you like the water?" Richardson asked.

"Water?"

"Just wondered if you would be interested in rafting down the Harvie Passage. Since you live close to it. People often don't take advantage of the facilities that are closest to them."

"Me… no, I'm not really interested in boating or watersports. I know the Canoe Club is close too, just off of the trails where I walk Stella. But I don't think I'll be taking any lessons."

He gave her a look, then nodded and continued to navigate around the many park walkers. It had been a cool day, and Margie was surprised that there were so many people out in the park. But apparently, they knew enough to dress in layers and be prepared for changes in the weather. Calgary was notorious for its change-able weather. Margie thought she had seen flakes of snow that morning when she took Stella out. It seemed awfully early in the year for snow, and she hoped that winter would hold off for another month or two.

She could see the pale blue river off to her left as they drove through the hills. Margie thought they were traveling roughly west.

"That's the Bow," Richardson said, nodding to the river. "Same river as goes past Pearce Estate Park. And Fish Creek Park, for that matter."

Margie imagined boating all the way from Glenbow Ranch Park, though the city, out to Fish Creek Park. It made her a little queasy thinking about it. All of that water rushing downstream. The picture that Richardson had put into her mind of a body tumbling over and over at the old weir. Her throat felt like it would close up just thinking of all of that water over her head.

"You don't think this murder is related to the body out at Fish Creek Park, do you?" Richardson inquired.

"No. We caught the killer in that case. I don't think it's related in any way, other than the fact that the body was discovered in a park."

"And he was stabbed."

"Right. But that's not particularly unique. Lots of people get stabbed."

He nodded in agreement. "True."

They started going uphill again, into an area more heavily treed. The pathway was narrower and gravel rather than paved. "This is part of Tiger Lily Loop. A short loop. Nice for families. You avoid the steep hill that you need to use to get to the rest of the park."

It was still pretty hilly. Margie studied the landforms and vegetation with interest and looked up to the sky to watch birds wheeling around them.

"If you're lucky, you could see our osprey. It's quite something to see them diving into the water for fish."

"Wow, yes. What other kinds of animals do you have out here?"

She was glad that the dead body was, as far as anyone had said, a fresh kill, and had not been subject to predation. There must be some large predators in the park, considering its size.

"Plenty of different birds and insects. There are bee and bird counting programs. Ground squirrels—you know, gophers. Badgers. Coyotes. Porcupines. Mule deer. You'll see the cattle; they still graze the park lands as part of the vegetation management program. There is an occasional bear sighting and we are on the lookout for cougar. But there haven't ever been any attacks on humans. The animals will do their best to avoid people and dogs."

Margie hung on as the cart climbed a steeper part of the trail. They were into the shadows of the trees and there were fewer hikers around.

Then they reached the yellow tape. Richardson hit the brakes and parked the cart. "Here we go."

Margie climbed out. There were a couple of conservation officers and RCMP uniforms. Margie nodded at the nearest RCMP officer. He was wearing a gray shirt similar to the conservation officers', with a tactical vest.

"Detective Pat?"

"Yes."

"Good to see you. I'm Sergeant Shack. You've been briefed?"

"I don't know much, other than the fact that there was a stabbing victim, similar to the Fish Creek murder that we just put away."

He nodded. "Not many details to give you at this point. You want to come have a look?"

"That's what I'm here for."

She stopped to put on protective gear to keep her from contaminating the crime scene, and they worked their way around the perimeter of the tape rather than through the middle. Margie took each step carefully, eyes alert for anything that might be evidence, even outside the tape. Then they ducked under the tape and moved toward the center of the cordoned-off area.

"Male, mid to late thirties," Shack said. "Doesn't appear to be robbery. No sign of a fight, no one has come forward who witnessed an argument or violence between the victim and someone else."

Margie nodded. Similar to the Fish Creek murder. She studied the body. The man was on his back so she could see the location of the stab wound. "I might be wrong, but I think the point of entry is a bit higher than the one in Fish Creek," she said. She leaned closer to get a better look at the body without touching it or compromising anything else at the scene. "Hard to judge his height and the angle of entry from this position."

"Your suspect in the Fish Creek case..."

She raised her brows at Shack. "Yes?"

"It was a juvenile offender?"

"Yeah. Tall for a fourteen-year-old, but still not an adult. How long ago, do you think?" Margie had nitrile gloves on. She touched the man's wrist to gauge his temperature. She couldn't feel any warmth through the thin layer of protection. It hadn't just happened. But she knew it had been over an hour since the Calgary police had been called in. Presumably, it had taken some time to sort out who should be involved in the investigation, and the family with the toddler had not reported seeing or hearing any violence, so the body had probably been lying there for some time before they saw him.

"Medical examiner will give us a better idea," Shack said. "I'm not sure yet. There's no predation or significant insect activity, so probably not long. It's close enough to the trail that you would think someone would have noticed him within a couple of hours."

"Definitely today."

"Oh yeah. Maybe early morning, but I'd be more inclined to think that it happened while the park was open. The conservation officers are pretty good at keeping people off of the park until it opens. You can't catch everybody, of course, but there's only one public lot, and not many people hike in."

Margie looked back in the direction of Calgary. "That would be quite a hike."

"Pretty impossible to come in from Calgary, actually. You need to take the highway, because there's no trail access through Haskayne Park yet. Eventually, there will be, but for the moment, Glenbow is cut off from the Calgary trail system." He pointed the other direction. "Cochrane, on the other hand, is only a couple of clicks away, and there are some pathways into the park from there."

Margie pulled out her notebook and made a couple of notes. "And those pathways would not be patrolled."

"Not likely. Checked now and then, but the CO's are going to be focusing on the public parking area."

Margie looked around. "How many people come through this trail during the day?" It seemed unlikely that a murder had been committed while people walked by on the trail. It would take a pretty bold murderer.

"You'll have to get those details from the CO's. They might

have some video footage too. But it's not busy. You can often walk this area and only see a few other visitors. It's relatively remote."

"The family that found him, are they still around?"

"They had a kid. Couldn't stay around for long, but they left their information. You can call or go see them."

Shack pulled out his notebook and relayed the contact information he had taken down from the witnesses. Margie wrote it in her own book.

"Did the child see…?"

"No. I don't think so. Didn't seem to be upset about anything except having to sit around while the grown-ups talked instead of exploring."

"Good. You always worry about trauma."

"If she saw him, she probably didn't understand what was going on. Just that someone was sleeping in the grass." Shack looked at the body. "I mean, it's not horrific."

"No. You're right." Margie could make out the hole that the knife had made and the darker areas of the shirt where blood had soaked into it. No pools of red blood or gore.

They could hear a vehicle approaching and all turned to look for it. In a few moments, a white van came into view.

"Medical Examiner's office," Margie observed. "Hopefully, they'll have a few answers for us."

CHAPTER THREE

Suited up and masked, Dr. Kahn from the Medical Examiner's office took a cursory look at the body, then looked at Sergeant Shack and Margie.

"Whose scene is it?"

"Calgary's," Margie said. "That's me."

"Okay. Nobody's touched the body?"

"I touched his wrist. Gloves on. Conservation officers and RCMP were here before me."

Shack took a few minutes to run through the steps since the body had been discovered with Dr. Kahn to establish the integrity of the scene. Kahn went through the motions of checking the body for any vital signs.

"Body is in rigor," he observed. "No pulse or respiration. Cool to the touch. I'll take ambient and liver temps. Looks like he's been here for a few hours."

Margie nodded. They would narrow it down more once the medical examiner had run through all of the usual protocols. And perhaps there would be video, like there had been at Fish Creek Park, to establish the time that the victim had arrived on the trail.

"Is there any identification on the body?"

Dr. Kahn took a brief look at the stab wound before moving

the man's clothing and feeling for a wallet. It was there in a zipped jacket pocket. Kahn passed it across to Margie. She examined it closely before opening it, looking for any trace that they needed to preserve. Then she opened it, keeping her gloved fingers on the very edges.

"David Smith."

"Well, great," Shack grumbled. "There are only a few hundred of those in Alberta."

"He's got a driver's license, so we have his address and date of birth." Viewing the card through the display window, Margie calculated the date in her head. "Age thirty-eight." She looked at the edges of the cards that peeked above the card slots. "Looks like Visa, Air Miles, Bank of Montreal access card, and AMA."

She displayed them to Shack, and he nodded his agreement. Margie didn't pull any of them out, and didn't pull out the plastic card accordion file she could see tucked into the next section. The forensic team would want to handle those, check for fingerprints and any other trace evidence.

Margie thumbed the cash section open to see a couple of bills. Blue and purple. "Fifteen dollars in cash."

She took an evidence bag from her shoulder bag and put the wallet into it. "Anything else in his pockets? Keys? Business cards? A list of people who might want to kill him?"

Shack snorted in amusement. Dr. Kahn didn't crack a smile. "Keys. Water bottle. Phone."

"Is there phone service coverage out here?"

"From my experience, yes, most of the park has coverage," Shack advised. "The exception being a blind spot as you get to the top of Glenbow Road. That's the gravel road you drove in on. Right at the top where you'd expect the coverage to be the strongest, it completely cuts out."

"Weird. Just today, or all the time?"

"As long as I've been coming here."

"Do you come here a lot?"

"Yeah. A couple of times a month, usually. I like to walk, take pictures."

"That's nice. You must live close."

He didn't answer at first, but when Margie kept looking at him, eyebrows raised, he realized that she expected an answer and it hadn't just been rhetorical. "Uh, yes. I'm just over in Tuscany."

"I'm new to Alberta. Is that in Cochrane or Calgary?"

"Calgary. West side. Did you see the Mormon temple as you drove out? White spire with an angel on top."

"Yes."

"When that's on your right, Tuscany is on your left."

"Oh, okay. That is nice and close. I'm not sure, but I'm thinking it's going to take me an hour to get home from here."

"I probably wouldn't be coming every week or two if I was that far away. Especially city driving." He gave a shudder. "I'm a country boy at heart. Southern Alberta farmland."

"Is that like this? Or prairie?"

"Prairie. Definitely. You can grow some crops around here. You'll see a couple of fields across the river growing canola or other crops. But it's hilly, so mostly this is ranching country—cows—rather than food crops."

"I'm from Manitoba."

"Ah, so you're used to flat. Yeah. Southern Alberta is more like that. Glenbow is mostly riparian. River and foothills."

THE SUN WAS GETTING low in the sky by the time David Smith's body was loaded into the medical examiner's van and the forensic tech had finished going over the ground with a fine-toothed comb looking for any possible evidence in the case.

"There isn't a lot to find," a technician named Joe said apologetically. "Looks pretty clean. The ground hasn't been trampled. There isn't any litter. It's a stab wound rather than a gun, so there aren't any shell casings to look for. No sign of the weapon here. The killer must have taken it with him."

Margie remembered Abdul, the killer in the Fish Creek case, casually pulling a hunting knife out of his hoodie pocket when asked about it. It had been cleaned and well-maintained, but they had been able to find traces of blood in the hinges and in the hoodie itself. No matter what anyone said, she knew that Abdul could not have been David Smith's killer, and that he had been Jerry Robinson's killer. There hadn't been a DNA match on the blood evidence yet, but there was blood on the knife. Abdul had not just confessed to murder for attention. The confession had not been coerced. He reacted as he'd been trained to, killing the man who had confronted him in the park. He thought it a perfectly natural reaction and the only way to protect himself from possible violence.

Darkness started to gather, the chill in the air deepening. The medical examiner's van was gone. The forensics team was gone. She and Shack and the others who were still there removed the yellow tape perimeter, looking one last time for anything that might have been missed. None of them found anything.

"You'll check for video evidence and send it on to me?" Margie asked Richardson, continuing the conversation they'd been having while the forensic experts were combing the ground for any other evidence. "Parking lot, trail cams, wildlife cams, whatever you've got. You never know how it might be helpful."

"Sure," Richardson agreed. "We'll go through it in the morning, make sure you get a copy."

Margie kept her mouth shut and didn't tell him that he needed to get it to her that night, and not wait until morning. But what did it matter? She wasn't going to look at it until morning anyway. As long as he got it to her, she didn't have anything to complain about.

He gave her an amused look, and Margie suspected that her irritation had been clear even with her face mask. Sometimes her emotions were too transparent.

CHAPTER FOUR

$\mathcal{M}$argie's estimate that it would take her an hour to get home from Glenbow Park had not been far off. She followed her GPS directions, which seemed to take her all the way around the north end of the city. But the speed limit was mostly one hundred and there was no significant traffic, so she really couldn't complain about the route it had selected.

She paused for a moment before unlocking the front door. She did her best to mentally push the homicide aside, walling off all of her questions and theories. Tomorrow would come soon enough and she didn't want to be crabby with Christina or to bring her down with her own mood. She took a couple of controlled breaths, then turned the key in the lock and opened the door.

"I'm home!"

There was a thunder of running feet, and Margie braced herself for the full weight of her dog, excited about seeing her after a long day apart.

"Who's a good girl? Were you a good girl? Were you good for Christina?" Margie scratched Stella's soft brown ears and kissed the top of her head, trying to calm the excited animal. "Such a good girl. Yes, you are."

Christina was at the kitchen table with her school books

spread out around her, but she was on her phone rather than working studiously on her textbook and computer. She waved at Margie, but made no sign that she intended to break off the call.

Margie took another deep breath, reminding herself not to be impatient with her teenager. She petted and scratched Stella some more, then went to the fridge. She'd had a granola bar in the car, but otherwise had not had any supper. Not that there was very much in the fridge. She hadn't gotten into the habit of cooking. Things had been too disrupted since moving to Calgary. Getting everything unpacked and in order, registering Christina for school, visiting with Moushoom, solving the Fish Creek murder. It hadn't left much time to stock the fridge.

Christina shoved her books around on the table looking for something and came up with a half-package of fries from A&W, which she handed to Margie.

They were cold, but maybe they would give Margie the energy she needed to open a can of something. Margie smiled her thanks at Christina, pulling her mask off to make sure that Christina could see that her gift was appreciated. She squirted some ketchup on top of the fries and stood leaning against the counter. She nibbled the fries, checked her email using her phone, and waited for Christina to get off of her call. It sounded like she was talking to a school friend, but not about the homework scattered over the table.

That was okay. With the amount that Christina had complained about having to move to Calgary, and then how bad she had said things were at school, Margie would happily accept her daughter being distracted by a friendship for a bit.

After finishing the fries, she checked the fridge again, and then the freezer. There was ice cream. Fries and ice cream were not a healthy dinner, and she would never have let Christina get away with a meal like that, but she really didn't have the energy to make much else. She sliced a slightly-soft banana into a bowl—that was fruit, and fries were a vegetable serving—and then added a small scoop of ice cream. Dairy. And there was nothing wrong with a moderate amount of sugar. At least it wouldn't keep her up at night when she needed to sleep.

Christina finally got off of her call. She looked at Margie, brows raised. "Ice cream is not dinner."

"Do you want some?"

Christina laughed. "I already had some."

"I hope you at least had a burger to go with it."

"Veggie burger. Yeah."

"I'll be sure to take Stella out for a long walk. Burn off the extra calories."

"I already took her out. And it's dark; you said not to go out after dark."

Margie looked for an excuse why it was okay for her to do, but not for Christina. "Well... I don't know; it will still be dark in the morning if I take her out before work."

"Safer early in the morning than late at night."

"It's not that late yet."

Christina gazed at her.

"Fine," Margie sighed. "But I'm the one who's supposed to be parenting you, remember?"

"Grover says hi."

"Grover?"

"Whatever his name is. Oscar."

"Oh, Oscar." Oscar was a man in the neighborhood who often walked his dog Milo on the pathway when Margie and Christina walked Stella. "Well, hi back, the next time you see him."

CHAPTER FIVE

*T*he video from the park wasn't in yet the next morning, so Margie checked the server to see what other evidence might have been processed by the medical examiner's office or forensics department. She would need to give a briefing on the Glenbow Park murder to the homicide team that morning, and so far there wasn't much to tell them. It might be a look-alike to the killing in Fish Creek, but the parallels were very general and could simply be a coincidence. How many people were normally stabbed in and around Calgary in a month?

Pictures of the contents of the wallet and the man's pockets had been posted to the workspace for the David Smith murder. She paged through them one at a time, looking at each of the cards and bits of paper in the wallet. It all seemed pretty routine. The usual bank and credit cards and customer loyalty cards. The cash that she had noted, a five and a ten. A scrap piece of paper with a woman's name and number on it. A photo of what looked like a high school, with kids in the distance. Maybe he had a kid in school. A club membership card and a rec club card. No sign of anything illegal or alarming.

The contents of his pockets were not much more enlightening. House and car keys. Loose change. Cough drops. Parking ticket stubs. The same type of stuff as she would expect anyone to have in their pockets.

She reviewed the pictures of the crime scene carefully, looking for anything that she hadn't noticed while she was there. There was no medical examiner's report yet, but she hadn't expected there to be. The body had been logged in, that was all.

Margie sighed. She went through her notes and thought through the various angles. They would need confirmation that it could not have been the same killer as the Fish Creek murder. She looked up the number for the Young Offender Center and gave them a call. Identifying herself as a law enforcement officer, she explained that she needed to know whether Abdul James was still in custody.

"Just a moment," the phone receptionist said politely. Margie could hear computer keys tapping rapidly, and then a pause while she waited for the results to display. "And the answer is… yes. Abdul James is still in custody."

"And you're sure he couldn't have been released or… wandered off. Sorry to be such a stickler about it, but sometimes these things do happen, and I need to reassure my investigative team that there is no way he could have been involved in this incident yesterday. No day release?"

The receptionist spent some more time looking through the records, tapping her keys briefly now and then. "No. I don't see anything. He's definitely still here and hasn't had any kind of day pass or work release. He hasn't even been out for court or medical care. Nothing that would have taken him out of the building."

"Good. That's very helpful, thank you."

By the time she got off the phone, she could see the others gathering in the briefing room for their morning "stand-up" meeting. Margie took her notes with her and joined them. Using the computer in the boardroom, she displayed a couple of pictures of the scene and the evidence on the big screen.

"How are things going?" asked Kaitlyn Jones, a blond, round-faced detective. "Were you very late getting home yesterday?"

"Later than I would have liked. But that's gonna happen when you have a murder. Couldn't very well leave it until today. Some coyote might have dragged off the body."

Jones's eyes widened. "Really?"

Margie laughed. "No, I think it would take several of them together, or a bear, to drag away a full-grown man. More likely they would just... eat in rather than take out."

Jones made a face. "Gross, Patenaude."

Margie knew that Jones had seen plenty of murder scenes, many of them more gruesome than an outdoor scene with animal scavenging. But she was still sensitive enough to be disgusted by Margie's suggestion. Or at least to pretend to be disgusted.

"So, anything helpful at the site?" Jones looked at the pictures on the screen.

"We'll go over that in a few minutes. But... not really. Nothing yet. And it was a pretty straightforward stabbing; I don't think they're going to find anything on the post."

Staff Sergeant MacDonald entered the room and everyone straightened up and stopped their conversations. Mac, a tall, gray-haired man with a military bearing, looked around to make sure that everyone expected was present.

"Good morning, all. Detective Patenaude, why don't you brief us on the new case?"

Margie nodded. She outlined the basics and indicated the pictures on the screen. There was little to tell them. "And I have checked with the Young Offender Center about Abdul James. He was definitely in custody all day yesterday and could not have been at Glenbow Park." She shrugged. "Not that I thought he had anything to do with this from the beginning."

"No," MacDonald agreed. "I don't think any of us did, but it is a little disconcerting to have two such similar cases so close together. Where do you plan to go next?"

"I'm waiting for video surveillance and the postmortem. Maybe those will help to narrow the investigation for us. We have his driver's license; I will start to track down his friends and family.

Ask questions. See if he was dealing with someone in his life who might have done something like this."

MacDonald nodded. "I doubt that this was a random thing. It will be someone that he had regular contact with. An ex or his ex's new boyfriend. A family member. No sign of drugs or gang membership?"

"No. everything seems clean. And he has no record."

Margie looked around at the team for any other suggestions. But it was a reasonably straightforward stabbing. All she could do was go through the usual police work. Chances were, family and friends would have some idea of directions to look.

They went on to discuss other cases.

৯

DAVID SMITH'S GIRLFRIEND—ACTUALLY his fiancée—was absolutely baffled by the suggestion that he might have been killed by someone he knew. She dabbed at her eyes and blew her nose repeatedly, trying to stay in control of her emotions as she answered Margie's questions. Cathy Lin was an Asian woman with delicate features, several years Smith's junior, with short hair that framed her face. Margie sat on the other side of the conference room table, as far away as she could and still feel like they were having an intimate conversation rather than shouting across the room at each other. She would have to disinfect everything before interviewing anyone else, with all of the tears and mucus…

"I don't know anyone who would want to hurt David." Cathy sniffled. "He didn't have any ongoing arguments with anyone. He didn't have an enemy or an unhappy ex. He was just… David. He was quiet, got along with people. He wasn't involved in drugs or gambling. None of that makes any sense."

"Please don't think that we're accusing him of anything," Margie said. "We're just exploring all of the possibilities. It is very rare that someone does something like this randomly. The victim is almost always known."

"But it still does happen randomly." Cathy sniffled. "There are still... mentally ill people who hear voices telling them to stab someone. It doesn't have to make sense."

"Of course it is possible, but most killers do not have diagnosed mental illness. Hallucinations commanding people to hurt others are very rare. That's why you hear so much about them when they do occur. Because they are novel. Something that doesn't happen every day. Of course we will be looking into the possibility. But it is more productive for us to look at David's life and figure out if someone targeted him. I know it's a shock, and I'm sorry that we have to talk to you about it right now, when your grief is so fresh."

"It's okay. I don't mind. It's just that... I can't think of anything that would help you. I can give you the names or numbers of his friends and family, but there is no way any of them had anything to do with this."

"Did David walk in the park a lot?"

"Yes, he liked the outdoors. He likes to walk and be in nature. Liked. It's calming. He would relax at the end of the day or get out there in the early morning."

"Did you ever go with him? Did he have any walking partners?"

"Sometimes I would go with him on a Sunday, when I had more time, but not usually during the week. I couldn't get out of bed that early, and I don't like walking while it is dark."

"Did he have other people he went with?"

"No. Sometimes when I would go with him, he would see people that he knew. You know, he would wave and say 'that's Ken' or whatever. They were regulars that he saw other times. Some people were in the park all the time, walking or volunteering, and they got to know each other by name. But they were just acquaintances. Not anyone that he brought home for dinner or went out for a beer with."

Margie nodded. She took a minute to make some random

notes before pursuing her next question so that it wouldn't sound like an accusation. "He drank?"

"No. Not a lot. He would go out for a beer now and then. He wasn't an alcoholic. He never got drunk."

"And he never said anything to you about getting into a fight at the bar. An argument. Losing a darts game and someone got upset. Something that seemed overblown or that he was worried about."

Cathy took longer to think about it, really considering the question. Maybe she hoped to find an explanation that was simple and wouldn't point to anyone she knew. Something that made sense.

But she shook her head and dabbed at her eyes. "No. I don't remember him ever saying anything like that."

"Okay. If you think of anything, please let me know." Margie pressed one of her business cards into Cathy's thin, moist hand. "I'm so sorry for your loss."

CHAPTER SIX

*M*argie had dealt with enough grieving family members and friends for one day. She needed a break. Everyone had said the same thing anyway; they couldn't think of anyone that David Smith ever had a problem with. He was shy and kept to himself and was a genuinely nice guy. He enjoyed walking in the park and was recognized by many of the regular walkers there. No one knew of anyone he'd had an argument with, cut off in traffic, or beat out for a promotion at work. He hadn't stolen or slept with anyone's girlfriend. He didn't have a load of money put away that his next of kin would like to get their hands on.

They were all just grief-stricken and Margie really couldn't deal with it anymore.

She decided to learn more about the setting. Maybe what had happened to David Smith had to do with something that had occurred in the park. Perhaps Smith and his killer preferred their own company but had the same favorite place to sit and reflect. Maybe Smith had a memorial there for a family member and someone had disrespected it, or vice versa. People sometimes became possessive about places or about a certain set of rules being followed, even if it didn't make sense to an outsider.

She pulled up the Alberta Parks website and read through the details about how the park had been established by the Harvie family, following through on the legacy their father left, protecting his favorite place from encroachment by the city. There were facts on the names of the trails, the elevations, the hours of the Visitor Center.

Margie switched to a broader internet search to see what other information was available and found the Glenbow Ranch Park Foundation's site. There were a number of educational programs and opportunities being run. A review of the social media sites and image searches showed a wide variety of flora, fauna, land-forms, and old buildings and equipment that could be found in the park. There was a book on the history of the land, *Grass, Hills, and History*. Margie thought it might be a good idea to get a copy for herself to see what the history of the place was.

There was always the possibility of a land dispute. Someone who thought that the land should belong to him. Or maybe Siksiká lands or sacred sites that had been taken away from them.

She looked through the pictures of the old houses, school, and other buildings that had once graced Glenbow in its glory days. There had been a thriving village, a sandstone quarry, and many other services at one time. Now it was all gone.

Margie read it all with interest. She saved some of the files to the case workspace to refer back to later. While there was the possibility of a land dispute, why would someone kill David Smith over it? He didn't have any claim over the park or the land. He wasn't misusing it, just taking walks out there. If someone had a dispute, it would be more logical to aim it at the provincial government or the Foundation, or even the Harvie family members. Not a random park visitor.

Unless David himself had a bone to pick with someone about it. But from what his family and friends had said, she didn't think that was very likely.

She came across a treasure hunters site which claimed there were Indigenous artifacts still in the park, that there was something of value from the old quarry, or that one of the old residents of "Millionaire Hill" had buried money somewhere on the grounds to keep it safe. Margie read the remainder of the page. Maybe somebody had thought that there was something of value there. It wasn't very likely, but people loved to believe unlikely stories. Especially when finding treasure was a possibility.

Had David Smith found something? Or said that he knew where some priceless artifact was? If he was always walking the park, then who was more likely to have an idea of the location of a treasure or artifact?

She jotted down some notes. It probably wasn't anything, but it was a nice diversion from talking to the grieving family and friends.

After consideration, she called the number of the Visitor Center. It was answered by a cheerful female voice offering to help.

"I don't know if you can help me." Margie identified herself. "I am working on the investigation of the... death out your direction. I was just reading some information online about the possibility of artifacts or treasures in the park. I don't suppose you would have any information on that, do you?"

"Well..." the voice on the other end of the phone was hesitant. "We consider the natural features of the park to be its treasures. The plants and animals, the landforms and viewscapes... it's all very important to us and brings joy to our visitors. You can't put a price on that."

"Of course." Margie couldn't help smiling. "But you know that's not what I'm talking about. Nobody killed David Smith over a viewpoint. Are there other artifacts in the park? Things of monetary value?"

She didn't suppose there was any point in asking. If there were something known to be of value, then it would have been removed, not left in place.

"I suppose there are," the receptionist said. "We don't make public any of the archaeological sites where there may still be artifacts present, but we are aware of several sites with archaeological importance. There was a study done before the park was even formed, and there have been a number of follow-up studies since then by various organizations or students."

"What kind of sites?"

"I really can't discuss them. They are not disclosed to the public so that they won't be overrun. People wouldn't leave them alone if they knew where they were. We have taken our lessons from other parks."

"Indigenous artifacts?" Margie questioned. "Money or treasures from the old ranchers or townspeople? Something still in the quarry?"

"The only thing that was ever in the quarry was sandstone," the woman replied with a laugh. "And not even the highest quality sandstone, at that. It was used to build several of the buildings in downtown Calgary and the Legislature in Edmonton, but they found better quality sandstone elsewhere, and the quarry was turned to a brickworks. But then it too went under. There wasn't any way for Glenbow Village to survive without industry, and gradually people moved out until it was a ghost town."

Margie made a couple of notes in her notepad. The helpful visitor information lady had not answered whether there were any Indigenous artifacts or treasures from the old ranchers. What had they discovered on archaeological digs in the past? It was frustrating that they wouldn't release the information to her. She didn't have enough evidence that it was relevant to get a subpoena to demand copies of the archaeological studies. There might be some of the information she needed in the Glenbow history book, but she suspected that if it was not fit for public consumption when someone called the information line, it would have been kept out of the book too. Still... it might be worth looking and finding out some more information about the park's history. Then she would have a better idea of whether there were anything worth pursuing.

"So is Glenbow considered a ghost town?" Margie asked. "I

didn't realize that any of it was still standing. Do you have people exploring there?"

"The ruins of Glenbow are out of bounds. Visitors are not supposed to be on or in those ruins. We don't want anyone stepping on a rusty nail or having some other accident out there. It isn't safe. It's in our best interests to just keep people away from the townsite."

"How much of it can you still see?" Margie was still tapping in computer searches and paging through the various image results. On typing in 'Glenbow Village ruins,' she was presented with pictures of a house with a sagging roof and several chimneys or other brick or sandstone structures that remained of houses long since gone. "Hmm. Not very much, I guess."

"No. We only have one house still standing, and no one is allowed to go inside. That would be very dangerous. And we don't want any vandalism." Her voice lowered to a serious tone. "People have very little respect for historical sites."

"I'm not surprised to hear that." Margie remembered being a patrol officer, and the amount of graffiti and destruction they'd had to deal with in Winnipeg. It was sickening how little people cared about historical sites or even just the spaces they lived in. A lot of hard work went into building communities, and their appearance and reputation could be destroyed in a few minutes with a can of spray paint or a few bullets or kicks.

"Do you get a lot of vandals in the park?"

"Luckily, not a lot. We are far enough away from the city that people don't happen onto the park by accident. They have to plan to come out here and have transportation. And we have Conservation Officers patrolling the park and trying to keep any… unwelcome parties out of the park."

"Yes, I've met a few of your CO's. They seem to be very diligent and dedicated to the parks they patrol."

"Our CO's are some of our greatest fans. We have some of them out here even on their days off, just because they want more time to walk the park and just relax and recharge."

Margie felt a sense of longing to be home with her daughter and to take Stella out to the park for a walk. Even just that little strip of green space along the ridge of the irrigation canal meant something to her. She could see how the Conservation Officers would fall in love with the parks they spent so much time protecting.

"Do your CO's use the golf carts all the time, or do they do foot patrols?"

"They walk, use carts or trucks, or ride horses. Whatever is the best way to get to where they want to go."

"They ride horses?"

"Yes, we have a few horses in the park that they can take out as needed."

"That's awesome." Margie had only ridden horseback a couple of times, and she had loved it. She didn't know if it was in her blood, because of her ancestry, or if she just happened to enjoy it, but she wished that she lived somewhere she could ride occasionally. When she had some spare time. But so far, spare time was just about as rare in Margie's life as a horse to ride.

"If I was to come to the park tomorrow, do you think someone could give me a short tour?" she suggested. "I'd like to get a better sense of the scope of the park, and whether these archaeological sites might have anything to do with David Smith."

"Of course, someone would be glad to help you out. Let me just look at the schedule for tomorrow and make sure that we will have someone available with a cart." There was silence for a few minutes, then the woman was back. "Yes. I'll make a note of it here. If you will come by the Visitor Center in the morning, we can have someone help you out."

What were the chances that Margie was going to find anything related to David Smith's death on her little guided tour? Margie put them at slim to none. But she would at least get a ride around a beautiful park, and that was almost like taking a holiday.

CHAPTER SEVEN

*M*argie had not planned on just vegging out in front of the TV when she got home. She had lots of plans. After taking Stella for a walk, she and Christina would take some time to unpack the few boxes that were left. They would wash the windows, vacuum, and maybe she would make some of the phone calls that were way down on her list that she just hadn't been able to summon up the energy to make.

But she was wiped out at the end of the day, and a person had to take a break now and then to just rest and regenerate, didn't they?

"Mom? Mom!" It took several calls before Margie was roused from her deep meditation in front of the silver screen.

"Christina! I'm awake. What was that?"

"Mom, did you see the way Stella is acting? I think there might be someone in the back yard."

"What?" Margie blinked herself awake, shaking away the cobwebs with a quick twitch of her head. She looked across the kitchen to where Stella slunk at the back door, sniffing the crack on the bottom edge with great concentration. "Stella? What is it? Is there someone there?"

Stella looked up for a moment, regarded her, and then put her nose to the floor again to sniff the air coming in under the door.

"Can you see anyone out there?" Margie went into Christina's bedroom, which looked into the back yard. She held her face against the window, staring out into the darkness. She could see little more than darkness. But looking out the window with the light of the kitchen and living room glowing behind her, she was probably very visible to anyone who happened to be in the yard.

"Is there anyone there?" Christina asked in a hushed voice.

"Not that I can see. She might have just smelled a skunk. There are a lot of them around."

"Yeah." Christina giggled. "Every time I look at the community page, somebody is complaining about their dog getting sprayed by a skunk. So probably *not* the best time to let Stella out into the yard."

"Probably not," Margie agreed.

As she pulled back from the window, she thought she saw a movement. Just her own reflected image in the glass? Or had there been something else out there? Something or someone who waited until she had pulled back from the window and couldn't see out anymore?

Margie shook her head. She was tired, and if she let her imagination get away from her, she wouldn't be able to get any sleep. Every noise the house made would sound like someone breaking in.

They were in a safe place. Nothing was going to happen to them there. Stella would be barking if there were some sort of threat outside the door. She would go nuts if there were an intruder and she thought she needed to protect her pack.

"I don't think it's anything to be concerned about, hon," she told Christina in a calm voice.

Christina nodded and took it in stride, not doubting Margie's words. Margie went to the freezer, wondering if there were any ice cream left.

꙰

MAYBE BECAUSE SHE had been worrying about not being able to sleep, Margie ended up tossing and turning. It seemed impossible to find a comfortable position in her bed. She usually slept well. She worked hard, and she had a walk with Stella after she got home, and after unwinding for a while in front of the TV, she was able to get to sleep quickly after tucking herself in.

But it was different this time. She closed her eyes and then, a few minutes later, opened them, wondering why she had bothered to close them in the first place if she was not tired. She had so much to do. It was going to be a busy day the next day if she were going to make her way all the way back out to Glenbow Park for another look around and a golf cart tour.

Margie was wide awake. It wasn't like those super frustrating nights when she was so overtired that she couldn't find sleep. She felt perfectly awake. She had no desire to sleep or sense of sleepiness at all.

She got up quietly and checked to make sure that Christina was in bed with the light off and all of her devices tucked away for the night. She walked around and checked the locks on the door, even though she had done that as part of her regular get-ready-for-bed routine. Stella noticed that she was up and padded after her, sniffing at each of the doors studiously, gathering whatever information her prodigious nose could sniff out. Stella looked up at Margie and whined.

"I know," Margie said. "There's nothing to worry about. I just couldn't get to sleep. I know there isn't anything out there. I just needed... to be sure."

Stella made a noise halfway between a huff and a sneeze. Margie wiped off her wet ankle. "Gee, thanks. Do you think you could slobber on your own feet?"

Stella pushed her nose into Margie's hand, demanding pets and scratches. Margie scratched her ears. "Yes, you're a good girl. You're a good dog. Even if you do sneeze and drool on me."

Margie warmed up a glass of milk in the microwave. Not the way her grandmother would have made it but, hopefully, it would still do the trick. She and Stella took one last circuit around the house, looking out each window and making sure that everything was secure.

SHE WAS sure that would be the end of it. Just one of those nights when things seemed disrupted. When she woke up in the morning, everything would be just like normal and all of the unease of the previous night would have disappeared. But instead, Margie felt worse than ever when she forced herself to slide out of bed and get started on her day. There was a tension in her belly, a tightness like a knot. Margie looked in on Christina and was relieved to see her in her bed sleeping peacefully. She'd dealt with too many parents in the past who had put their children to bed at night, and when they got up in the morning, they were gone. Teenagers, usually, but sometimes younger schoolchildren or even toddlers. They wandered off sleepwalking or were abducted by spouses. They ran away or left to go to a party and never returned. The parents had to live with the guilt that went along with letting their child wander off in those few hours they were blissfully unconsciousness.

A person couldn't be vigilant all day. Margie couldn't protect her child from all evil influences. There were things she could never protect Christina from, no matter how hard she tried.

Margie started the coffee brewing. While she was trying to cut back and not have coffee every morning before breakfast—or *for* breakfast—she knew that she couldn't do without it after a night like that. She was going to need the caffeine to get her motor running.

Of course, caffeine didn't help with anxiety. In fact, it amplified it. She reminded herself as she breathed in the smell of the coffee as it brewed that she would probably feel worse in the afternoon. She would get an initial kick from the coffee, but she would have a mid-afternoon crash. Being so tired and anxious, it would probably be a doozy, and she needed to keep in mind that it was just because of the caffeine. It didn't mean that anything was really wrong with the world or that anyone was out to get her.

Stella was scratching at the back door to get out. Margie let her into the yard. She went into Christina's room, where she could see through the window that the back gate was still shut and latched.

"Hey, sleepyhead. Time to start getting up."

"Not yet," Christina groaned.

Margie was going to protest that Christina needed to get up and moving if she were going to catch the bus and get to school on time.

"You said I can choose what time to get up," Christina mumbled. "You said as long as I was getting to school, you wouldn't bother me."

She was right, of course. Margie was trying to allow her daughter the space to learn to be a responsible adult, and that meant that if she didn't choose to get up until ten minutes before the bus and ended up having to eat on the run and fly out the door in a panic, that was the natural consequence of her choice. As long as Margie didn't get reports from the school that Christina was late to or missing classes, Margie wouldn't enforce a specific bedtime or wake-up time.

"Okay. I just wanted to check the back gate. If you want to get a few more minutes sleeping, you can."

"'Night." Christina's long, even breaths resumed. Margie was impressed with Christina's ability to go back to sleep once she'd been awakened. She herself probably would have found it impossible to get back to sleep again and would have had to get up, whether she liked it or not. Margie went back to the kitchen to start on her coffee, then to the bathroom for a quick wake-up shower. If she got hers in early, she wouldn't have to fight

Christina for it later when there was no longer time for both of them to use it.

By the time she got back to her coffee , she could hear Christina stirring. She got up and used the bathroom. When she came into the kitchen, she ran her fingers through her tangled hair, blinking in the sunlight.

"Hi." Her voice was rough and sleepy still.

"Morning. Did you have a good rest?"

"Yeah, it was fine." Christina helped herself to a cup of coffee.

Margie bit her tongue and didn't say anything about it. She couldn't very well criticize Christina for drinking coffee when she herself did. Allowing Christina some privileges of adulthood helped Margie enforce more important rules, such as no alcohol. At least, Margie hoped it would work that way.

Christina took a few swallows of her coffee. She went to open the door when Stella barked to be let in.

"Mom!"

Margie moved quickly at Christina's cry of alarm. She saw Stella on the back step, mouth open in a pant, her muzzle bloody.

"Is she hurt?" Margie crouched down in front of Stella for a closer look. She pushed back Stella's lips to look at her teeth and gums and examined her nose and face for any sign of an injury. She'd heard of people tossing meat spiked with sewing needles into back yards to injure pets. She couldn't see any sign of injury on Stella. She looked around, scanning the yard for the source of the blood. If it didn't come from Stella, then...?

"There's something over there," Christina motioned to a dark mound Margie could just barely see.

Margie slid on a pair of garden clogs—one day, she was going to start gardening—and strode through the cold, wet grass to see what it was.

It took a minute for her to be able to recognize the lump of fur stippled with dark blood as a rabbit. She stared, trying to process it. Stella surely hadn't killed the rabbit. She chased rabbits sometimes when they were out for a walk, and Margie knew that she was hopeless at it. The rabbits always zig-zagged away, leaving her in the dust. Maybe if one were already sick or injured…

Her stomach was tied in knots. She knew there were city by-laws about vicious animals, including animals that had killed other animals, but she didn't know all of the details. She might have to look them up.

Margie looked more closely. She was a homicide detective; it didn't bother her to look at the dead body of a rabbit. Except it did. Just as looking at a human body always stirred deep emotions despite her need to remain impassive and to compartmentalize those feelings. She tried to look past the areas where Stella had worried at the body. Stella had not been hungry, but curious. Margie tried to figure out how the animal had died. Maybe it had been hit by a car and crawled into their yard. Or another animal had killed it.

But she saw a wound with straight edges.

That didn't make any sense. She remembered the squirrel they had found in the yard. Also dead. Also cut with something with a straight edge. Margie had explained it away to herself that time. The squirrel could have caught itself on something sharp. Animals did get hurt in the wild. Maybe there was a sharp can or a piece of abandoned equipment that she wasn't aware of. A lawnmower blade someone had put aside to clean and sharpen and then never followed up on.

But two dead animals in her yard with injuries caused by a straight edge was hard to explain. The first time she had picked up the body and discarded it in her compost bin. This time it was a bigger animal. Harder to ignore. Harder to explain away how a second dead animal came to be in her yard. It would be one thing if an animal had mauled them. Everyone would assume Stella had killed them. But Stella didn't carry a switchblade in her pocket.

"Mom? What is it?"

"It's just a rabbit, Christina."

"Did Stella—kill it?"

"No. I don't think so."

Christina stood on the back step, looking at her, waiting for her to explain further. But Margie didn't want to clarify unless Christina asked for more details. It was better if she didn't know. Christina didn't ask for more. Maybe she knew better from Margie's silence or her body language.

"Are you going to clean it up?"

"I'll do it a bit later. You'd better finish getting ready for school."

Christina looked down at Stella, still by her side. "What about Stella? Will you clean her up?"

Stella would probably eventually lick everything off. But it would be better if Margie wiped her muzzle and face with a towel so they didn't have to look at it or worry about Stella getting flecks of blood inside the house.

"Yes. Would you get me a towel?"

Christina nodded and went to get one.

CHAPTER EIGHT

*O*nce Christina was on the bus, Margie placed a call to her own department. MacDonald was in and was able to take her call.

"Detective Patenaude. How can I help you?"

"This is a personal matter, sir, but I wonder if you could help me out and tell me who to call. And to let you know that I won't be in until later today."

"What's up?"

Margie explained about the rabbit in her yard, and he wasn't too concerned about it until she described how both it and the previously discovered dead squirrel appeared to have been killed by a blade or sharp piece of metal and left dead or dying in her yard.

"You're sure they weren't killed by your dog."

"We've never had anything like this happen before. Of course she chases squirrels and rabbits, but she never catches them. I'm not a pathologist, but I don't see how a dog could leave marks like that. A clean incision. It's possible that once, it could just be some weird accident. I thought maybe a tin can or piece of sharp trash. But twice? Left dead in my yard both times? It wasn't the dog and it couldn't be a coincidence."

"Have you had any threats? Anyone been hanging around your yard? Any contact from someone you didn't want to have anything to do with?"

"No." Margie cast her thoughts back, trying to identify any threats she might have received, any anger that seemed inappropriate or weird behavior from anyone she'd arrested or had anything to do with since she got to Calgary. It wasn't very hard. She hadn't really had contact with that many people since arriving in Calgary. And the only person she had arrested was Abdul. She had talked to other people. But Abdul was the only one who she had taken into custody.

She remembered Abdul asking about her dog and looking at Stella's picture on her phone. Flipping through the pictures without asking, seeing Christina's photo too. A girl about his own age.

But Abdul was in custody. That had already been established.

"There's... Abdul's foster father. But he never made any threats or said anything inappropriate. He didn't even seem that upset, he just sort of took it in stride."

"He could have been masking deeper emotions. Sometimes it's the quiet ones who feel things the most. Do you want us to pick him up?"

Margie resisted. "No. I don't think it could be anything to do with him."

"Would he know about your dog? Where you live?"

"Well... it's a possibility. He was there when Abdul and I talked about Stella." She was embarrassed and tried to explain further. "I was trying to establish a relationship with him. To talk about how he might have come to be talking with Robinson. You know, two people out walking dogs start talking to each other about the dogs, the view, and so on. Maybe Abdul and Robinson might have struck up a casual conversation about the weather or the view or the fact that they had seen each other there a few times before."

"Are your phone number or address listed anywhere? Somewhere searchable? Do you find them if you Google search yourself?"

"I've been careful; I don't think so. I'll check."

"Did you talk about what area you live in? What it's close to?"

She tried to remember what else she might have revealed around Abdul or his foster father, Sadiq. "I don't think so, but I don't remember every word I said around them."

"It might be a good idea to check in on him, ask a few questions."

"Yeah. I'll think about that. Who should I call about this rabbit? Is there someone who will come and have a look and not just brush me off as a hysterical woman? I have a daughter. If one of us is being stalked…"

"Let me get you a name. I'll text it to you."

"Thanks. And I'll be late getting in today. Actually, I was thinking of going back to Glenbow Park today for a tour and another look around. Maybe I'll just go out there once I finish here? If I'm going to miss the stand-up meeting anyway, it's a lot faster to take Stoney Trail than to go through downtown rush hour traffic."

"Sure. I'll let everyone know that's where you are. And they can call you if they have questions or information you'll want to hear?"

"Yes. I'll be available on the phone. One of the guys I talked to at the park said there's only one place that has spotty reception; my phone should be working the rest of the time."

֍

THANKFULLY, the officer who came out to have a look at the dead rabbit and talk to her about what had happened was serious and engaged and didn't act like Margie was crazy for thinking that someone might be trying to send her a message. Constable Evans nodded and made notes and looked at the body of the rabbit, with flies starting to buzz around it. He pulled down his mask to speak to her, standing well back.

"I'm going to take this with me, if you don't mind. I agree that it doesn't look like it was killed by an animal or an accident, so we'll want to follow up and see if this is something to be concerned about. If we have some sicko out there killing animals then, even if he isn't specifically targeting you, there is still reason to be concerned."

Margie nodded. Everyone knew that killing or torturing animals could be the beginning steps of someone who would later turn to killing or torturing his fellow human beings. If they could catch him before he moved on to people...

She squirmed, anxious and sick to her stomach. She had just arrived in Calgary. She wanted her daughter to be safe. She didn't want to have to worry about some sicko who wanted to terrorize them or was just really enjoying his brutal hobby.

"Do you think...?"

"I think you were meant to find it," Evans said slowly. "If he was just randomly killing animals and throwing them over fences, then I wouldn't expect him to throw them into your yard twice in such a short period of time. If your neighbors were all finding dead animals in their yards, I think you would hear about it pretty quickly."

"Yes. We don't know everybody, but we do... say hello, talk over the fence, stuff like that. And there is a community Facebook page. If there were a lot of animals being killed, I'm sure it would have been mentioned there. Unless it just started."

"Maybe he'll move on to another area to avoid being caught, and this is all that you'll see."

"I hope so. I have a daughter. I don't want to keep finding things like this in the yard. She's here alone sometimes after school or if I have to go out to a crime scene. I want her to be safe being here alone."

"Of course. We'll look into it and see what we can find out. See if there are any similar reports anywhere else in the city, especially in this area. Have the lab examine the rabbit and see what they can tell us about it."

"I'm sorry I already got rid of the squirrel. I expect the bins have been emptied since then. And even if they haven't, it will be buried in there under everything else. I don't imagine the lab techs would be able to tell much about it in that state."

"Maybe if this was an episode of *Bones* and I was from the Smithsonian…" he teased. "But I'm not," he added seriously. "I wish I could tell you that the body is bound to give us the answer as to who is doing this, but I can't do that. Maybe it will tell us something, maybe nothing."

They grimaced at each other. Evans pulled out a business card. "You can call me directly if anything else happens. Even if you just have an insight or a random thought about who could be doing something like this. Call, text, or email."

Margie took the card. "Thanks."

He nodded. "I'll let you get on to work now. Good luck with your case."

CHAPTER NINE

The young man who met Margie at the Visitor Center introduced himself as Ian. Margie was surprised at how young he was. She had expected that, like at a lot of the museums and conservation areas she had gone to, the docents would be retired folks. People who still wanted to keep their hand on a pet project even when they were no longer able to work there.

"Ian. Nice to meet you. How long have you been working here?"

"A couple of years. Don't worry; I know all of the important stuff. If you have any questions I can't answer, we'll look them up when we get back or I'll find out the answer from someone who knows."

He opened the garage, and Margie saw several golf carts that hadn't been there when she had last seen it. Big carts for a lot of tourists, with a canopy sunshade overhead.

"Oh, I wasn't judging, just surprised that someone so young would be working here."

"We get a lot of kids. University students who are working on their thesises, looking for a summer job, wanting to do a particular study in the park. We have older guides as well, our park stewards in particular, but today you get me."

"And I'm sure you'll do a great job. This is a fascinating place. I was doing some research on the internet about it. There's really a rich history."

"There is," Ian agreed, climbing into one of the smaller golf carts and motioning for Margie to take the seat next to him. Margie sat down. He backed up, turned around, and off they went. He didn't take the same trail as Margie had taken the day of the murder, west to Tiger Lily Loop, but went the other way and, in a few seconds, they were nosing down a long, steep hill.

Margie hung on to the side of the cart and leaned back, but she didn't need to worry that it was too steep for the golf cart. Of course, Ian was used to driving up and down it all the time, and he didn't have any trouble controlling the cart or weaving slowly between various small groups of walkers, cyclists, and mobility scooters.

He smiled at her. "Downhill is easy. The hard part is always making sure you've got enough electricity to get back up the hill again."

"What do you do if you don't?"

"Walk. Or everybody walks except for the driver and, hopefully, he has enough electricity to get it up the hill without the extra weight of passengers. Otherwise, you're going to need to get a tow or a lift in the back of the truck, and that's pretty embarrassing. They'll call you 'Juice' to the end of your days because you ran out of juice."

Margie laughed. "That's cute. Is that your nickname?"

"Not mine." He crossed his fingers and looked heavenward. "Hopefully, it won't ever be."

After the hill, they traveled over a long, level trail out in the sun. It would be a challenging walk on a thirty-degree day.

"Is there running water in the park?"

"No. The washrooms are outhouses. And there are no water fountains. If you need water, you have to carry it in with you. There is bottled water available at the Visitor Center when it is open, but it isn't always open. If you've been here once, you generally remember after that."

"I guess so!"

She was silent, looking at the brilliant azure sky with barely a cloud in it. The trees in the direction of the river were starting to change into their autumn colors, pretty yellows dappled among the green. She watched the birds, butterflies, and bees flying among the flowers and bush beside the trail.

"There was frost this morning. I wasn't expecting such a warm day."

"September in these parts is very changeable. You can have frost overnight and twenty-eight or nine during the day. I don't think we'll see any more thirty-degree days this year, but you never know. We still could. What they used to call an Indian summer, before it became politically incorrect."

"Not that anyone in your generation ever called it that."

"No."

He pointed out several different topographical features for her and talked about the bee homes and bird and bat houses built to help preserve various species in the park. The special fescue grasses that were important in the sequestration of carbon. What people had done there when the village was still populated. He mentioned the cattle kept on the property that helped to keep the long grasses cropped down so that they wouldn't be a fire hazard.

There was a growing noise behind them. Margie searched the trees for the origin of the loud rumble. Ian slowed the cart to look, and pointed out the train that Margie could just see through the trees. "You'll be able to see it better in a minute. The CPR line runs through the park and is still quite active. We are part of the shipping route between the coast and Eastern Canada. The CPR line runs from coast to coast."

Margie knew some of the stories of the building of the railway. It had been an important development for Canada, helping to build a unified country. But it had been built on the backs of migrant workers under terrible work conditions, with four

Chinese workers being killed for every mile of the railway line through the Fraser Valley. Immigrant labor had just been a commodity, and the big corporations didn't particularly care how many lives were lost in building the railway, just as long as there were plenty more available. Building the railway had also meant moving Métis populations, which had led to the Red River Rebellion.

"What can you tell me about the Indigenous peoples who lived here and any artifacts left by them or the villagers?"

Ian looked at her sideways. "Are you…?"

Margie raised her eyebrows, waiting.

"Are you Native? I mean, you look a little like it…"

Margie chuckled. She patted at her bun, which kept her long, black hair coiled neatly away. Her face would rarely be mistaken for anything but Indigenous Canadian. Maybe Asian or mixed race if you squinted, but her Cree heritage showed.

"I am Métis."

"Oh, okay." He looked relieved that he hadn't put his foot in his mouth by thinking she was something she was not. "Do you come from around here?"

"Was this a Métis settlement?"

"Well, no. The people here are mostly Nakoda. There are other tribes as well, but it was the Nakoda who mostly settled along the Bow River here."

"No, I don't come from this area. I come from Manitoba."

"The Red River Rebellions and all that?"

"Yes. All that."

He nodded wisely. "Well, to answer your question, of course there were Native peoples on this land thousands of years before the white man. It is Treaty 7 land, and the Tsuut'ina Nation is just to the south. We have a good relationship with our neighbors, and they sometimes join us for special park programs and observances."

"So what kinds of things could you find around the park? Teepee rings? Arrowheads? Graveyards?"

"They can answer some of those questions at the Visitor Center. But we can't say too much about what archaeological sites there are in the park or where they are located, so that we don't have treasure hunters ripping stuff up and destroying it. We study what we can. In a very respectful way, following proper archaeological procedures."

"Do you get a lot of people who ask? Or people who wander around here on their own looking for treasures? Have you had much vandalism because of it?"

"We field questions about it pretty regularly," he agreed. "But we do what we can to discourage people from trying to find artifacts. It is destructive."

Margie watched as the vegetation and topography transformed around them again. Every few minutes, they went from one kind of tree dominating the landscape to another; the trail went out to the water and wound away from it again. The shaded areas were cool and the open areas made her break out into a sweat. It was such a varied landscape; she could see how walkers and bikers would want to see it again and again, exploring all of its different facets.

"Tell me some more about Glenbow Village."

He had pointed out the ruins that they had passed, but it was all too quick, and Margie wanted to get a better sense of it. She knew, in the back of her mind, that it really didn't have anything to do with her investigation, and she should finish up her tour of the park and get back to the office where she could continue her desk work. But it was nice just being out in nature, even if it was zipping by a little too fast.

Ian told her some more stories about the village as they continued, pointing out various pieces of their life that the former residents had left behind. Wagon wheels and the shell of a motor car. The old quarry and brickworks. He talked about the school and how it had been moved and preserved.

"This is as far as we are going to go," he told her as they

approached the Narrows. "I'll just get turned around, and we'll head back."

"And the trails don't continue through to Calgary?"

"Not yet. But someday soon…"

"Is there a projected date?"

"There are plenty of projected dates. They are doing work on the Haskayne Park access right now. So hopefully *soon*…"

Margie nodded. She knew how city projects could drag on for years. Building and developments promised, infrastructure that had been projected for years and still wasn't anywhere in sight. They couldn't be prepared for all of the changes in the economy. For a downturn in development due to red tape. For the pandemic. Who could ever have predicted the way 2020 alone would unfold?

She recognized the trail as they got close to the steep access hill. "Can I get back to Tiger Lily Loop from here?"

"Yes." He looked at his watch. "But I can't take you there. I have to be back for a scheduled tour."

"That's okay. If you can just point me in the right direction, I can get there. I'd just like to take another look around and to… walk the victim's footsteps, if you know what I mean. Maybe something will occur to me that hasn't before."

"Well, of course you're welcome to walk around and have every right to be investigating up there, so have at it. Just take this trail." He pointed. "Watch for a branch to the right, take that trail, and then you'll be on Tiger Lily Loop. You can go either direction and it will get you back up to the top where the access to the parking lot is. There is a map, so you can stop and look and orient yourself if you're not sure. Or ask someone else who looks like they know where they are going. We have a lot of visitors who come back multiple times and know their way around the park very well. Okay?"

"Yes, that sounds good." Margie looked along the trail but couldn't see where it branched off. But it sounded very straightforward. "Thanks very much for the tour and all of the information. I don't know that it will help at all with the case, but it has certainly made me want to come back for another visit, and to bring my daughter with me next time. Maybe my dog too."

There had been lots of dogs amongst the walkers that she had seen. She knew that there was a leash rule, which was fine with her. Stella was happy to be on a leash, and it would ensure that she didn't chase after any of the ground squirrels or the cattle or a moose or something else that could do her harm.

Ian waved goodbye and turned up the steep pathway to the top.

Margie started out along the trail.

It was afternoon and she hadn't had lunch. She'd barely had breakfast. She had only walked about a kilometer when she realized that she should not have started out without a bottle of water. No food in her system and no water with her, the sun beating down on her on a trail that had minimal tree cover. Not a very good idea if she wanted to complete her walk quickly and still get back to the homicide department to do more work there before the end of the day. All in all, she was afraid it was going to be a wasted day, having gotten no closer to tracking down David Smith's killer.

She shook her head and kept walking, but at a reduced pace. She didn't want to overheat and overstress her body trying to get the walk finished too quickly. One step at a time at a steady, leisurely pace, and she would eventually come out on top and wouldn't be too much worse for wear.

Bicyclists whizzed by her in both directions. She saw walkers of all shapes, ages, and descriptions, from fit-looking oldsters with neatly pressed clothing and wide-brimmed hats to young people in skimpy outfits showing off brilliantly tattooed bodies. Mothers with little children, retirees and amputees on electric scooters; it seemed like everybody had chosen that day to be out enjoying one of the last hot days of the year in the park.

Margie wiped her sweaty forehead and neck and kept going. She hadn't even thought to bring a hat with her. She hardly ever needed a hat; she was never out in the sun long on her walks with Stella and, with the shortening days, the sun was usually too low in the sky both in the morning and the evening to worry about exposure.

She stopped and looked back behind her and then ahead of her. She didn't see any sign of a branching trail. Had she somehow missed it? She didn't see how she could have. She had stopped at a map and looked over it but, to her shame, Margie was terrible at the spatial planning and memory needed to read a map and keep it in her head as she walked. She tried turning on her phone and looking at Google Maps, but the paths were not well marked and were not labeled, so she couldn't be sure if she were on the correct route or not.

She reached a lookout and stood there for a few minutes, looking at the mountains in the distance, the trees beside the river, and a stone chimney jutting up toward the sky. It was not the same view as she had been able to see from Tiger Lily Loop. She was pretty sure she had missed her turn. She didn't know if the trail she was on would eventually loop around and return her to the place she had started with Ian. Even if it did, she was pretty sure she had covered about three kilometers already, and she really didn't want to guess how much farther it would be. She swore under her breath. She turned around and retraced her steps, trying to remember what the turnoff Ian had taken had looked like so she wouldn't go too far back again, but could get up the steep hill and to her car in the parking lot and not keep wandering into the middle of the park, where she might eventually have to call to have someone rescue her.

Ian had told her to watch for the branching trail to her right so, having turned around, it would be on her left. She mentally reviewed both hands and clenched the left so she wouldn't get confused as to which side the branch would be on.

CHAPTER TEN

*M*argie was relieved when she found the trail that broke off to her left. The tension in her shoulders and abdominal muscles relaxed, and she felt like she was in control again. She enjoyed the view, smiled and nodded at other walkers, and stepped forward with confidence. She would check out the loop, satisfy herself that she hadn't missed anything—or alternatively, gain some insight that they had not had before—and she would still have some time to go back to the office to review any other evidence or leads that had come in during her absence. She might be a little late getting home, but Christina would be fine on her own for a couple of hours.

Margie's stomach tightened again when she remembered the squirrel and the rabbit and the possibility that someone was stalking and threatening her. She didn't want to be late getting home. She didn't want Christina taking Stella out for a walk alone. A dog was good defense, and people wouldn't usually attack someone accompanied by a large dog. But it didn't always hold. There was still the possibility that someone would recognize Stella's true wuss nature and not be worried about her reaction. Or they would bring a knife or a gun and be ready to take her out. Or a piece of meat spiked with poison or sewing needles.

She picked up her pace. She shouldn't be wasting so much time walking around the park. Her tour hadn't given her any insight into whether the killer or Smith might have been some kind of treasure hunter, maybe rivals in hunting artifacts. It had been a long shot, but she had hoped that being there would provide the key piece of information that she needed to solve the case.

Nothing on the pathway looked familiar. But Margie had come onto it a different way than she had previously. Or was it the same route as she had taken when Richardson brought her in on the golf cart, and it was just her perspective or speed that made it seem foreign? Margie scanned the scenery, not seeing the beauty anymore, just desperately looking for something that resonated with her. Something familiar that would reassure her that she was on the right path. She had taken her first left, so it should have been the Tiger Lily Loop. She'd missed it the first time but, when she had reversed, coming back from the tall, ominous-looking chimney, she had taken the correct turn. She was sure of it. Ian had said to take the right, and she had reversed direction and taken the left.

For a long time, she didn't see anyone else. The trail dipped down when she had expected it to continue to rise. The trees didn't look right. Nothing looked right. A couple of cyclists whizzed by her, too fast for her to flag them down or ask any questions. Finally, she saw a woman neatly dressed in khakis and a white hat coming toward her, a trekking pole in each hand.

"Excuse me…" Margie stopped her.

"Yes?"

"Is this Tiger Lily Loop?"

"Oh, no, dear. This is the Badger Bowl. Tiger Lily Loop is that way." She gestured back behind Margie.

"Are you sure? I was following the directions that the young man from the Visitor Center gave me…"

"Yes, I'm sure. The trail heads are quite close together; it's easy to mistake them."

Margie turned and looked back the direction she had come, heart sinking. She kept taking the wrong turns. She was going to have walked a half-marathon by the time she got back to the parking lot. On an empty stomach and no water.

"Are you okay, dear? The Badger Bowl is still a nice walk. I'm sure you'll enjoy it."

"I need to be on the Tiger Lily Loop. That's where... I'm a police detective, and that's the one I'm supposed to be checking out."

"Oh, I thought the police were finished with all of that. Didn't you get everything you needed earlier?"

"We gathered all of the evidence. I'm just looking for... inspiration, I guess."

The woman smiled, her wrinkles curving gently upward. "Well... you'll get out of the Bowl faster if you go back the way you came than if you continue around the loop. If you don't mind walking with me, I can show you which way."

"That would be really helpful, actually. I'm so turned around. I don't know the park, and I thought it would be simple to get from one place to another, but I'm not good with directions."

"Not everyone is," she agreed placidly. "My name is Joanne. I'm not fast, but I know my way around. So if you just stick with me, I'll get you to where you need to go."

"I really appreciate that."

They started walking, Margie turning around to go back the way she had come. She sighed. "It really is a beautiful place. I wish I was here for a reason other than the investigation, so I could enjoy it."

"You'll have to come back sometime when you can just relax and take it all in. Or take one of the cart tours. The park is pretty big, but the cart tours can get you from one end to the other so you can get a better idea of the scope."

"I took a quick tour today. It is pretty impressive."

"There's a lot to see."

"Do you know of any artifacts or anything valuable in the park?"

Joanne considered. "Its value is its history and all of the diverse species in the park. Not in anything of monetary value. The park land itself is worth millions. But you can't put it in your pocket and sell it on the street."

"No." Margie made a face that Joanne couldn't see behind her mask. She was puffing a little as she went up the hill again. Joanne seemed to be breathing just fine, keeping a steady rhythm with her trekking poles. Margie was probably just breathing hard because of her anxiety and the feeling that she had to get to the Tiger Lily Loop quickly, even though she didn't expect to find anything there.

"I was so sad to hear about David Smith," Joanne said. "You're investigating the stabbing?"

"Yes. Did you know him?"

"Not well. Just to say hello when we passed each other in the park. He seemed like a nice man. He cared about the park and his health. Like most of us here. We are all doing what we can to stay active, to take care of ourselves and the environment. Getting time in nature is very important. You can't sit in front of electronic screens all day without negative effects. I like my Netflix as well as the next person, but you need to take a break regularly to get your dose of nature and fresh air."

Margie nodded. She felt guilty that she hadn't been able to exercise very much lately, but she was just settling in with a new job. She would find more time. She was walking Stella every day or twice a day. Not long walks, maybe, but it was something.

"I guess I don't need to tell you about the benefits of nature," Joanne said, giving a little laugh. Margie looked at her.

"What do you mean? I mean—I do try to get out, but I'm not sure why…"

"Because you're Indian, I mean. Or whatever the politically correct term is these days. You are, aren't you? I'm glad to see that someone like you is able to get onto the police force. You always hear about racism and how people like you can't get into anything but physical labor."

"Oh. Yes, thank you. And you're right; I was raised to love and respect nature. I don't spend as much time as I should, but I love to be out here." Margie made a motion to include all of the plant and animal life around her.

She thought of Moushoom. She needed to go see him too. Maybe she could take him from his little apartment over to the pathway along Twenty-Sixth Street where she walked Stella. He would probably really like that. She was sure he needed the exposure to nature too. Probably more so than she did. He had grown up in a much more traditional lifestyle, where he had been much more in touch with nature than she had. Maybe that was why he had a much better sense of direction than she did.

Or maybe that was just something about the brain she was born with. While her Cree progenitors probably had an excellent sense of direction, who knew about the early explorers? How many of them had just happened to stumble upon their discoveries because they had no idea where they were going?

She realized that she and Joanne had stopped talking and were just walking in silence. She felt suddenly awkward. "Sorry. Did you ask something?"

"No. Just enjoying the quiet."

"Oh. Okay. Me too. I don't do this very often."

She relaxed as they walked, listening to the rhythm of their feet. They would get there when they got there; there was no point in her getting all wound up about getting back to the office at a specific time. If there were anything urgent, someone on the team would call her. She pulled out her phone to make sure that she still had power and coverage. Both appeared to be strong. They could get her if they needed her.

Eventually, they reached the trailhead.

Joanne pointed. "This is the one you need to follow," she said, indicating the gravel pathway and tracing its directions in the air in front of them. "You can go either way, it's a loop and they will both get you to the parking lot eventually. You're about halfway, so you can take the one you want."

Margie tried to remember which she had taken with the conservation officer to get to the murder scene. She thought it was the left.

"Thank you so much for your help. Who knows how long I would have been wandering if it wasn't for you."

"Oh, someone else would have helped you. You only have to ask. Chances are, the person you ask will know the way. If they don't, just ask the next one. Most of the visitors come regularly."

"I appreciate it. Thanks."

Margie started up the left leg of the trail. "And I can't get lost from here, right? There's no way I'm going to end up in the Badger Bowl again?"

"No. You'll either end up in the parking lot or back here again. Those are the two connection points. And it's pretty hard to miss the parking lot. There's a big sign." Her eyes crinkled as she smiled. "A whole bunch of parked cars."

Margie laughed. "Thank you. Have a great day."

"I will. You too."

Margie breathed a sigh of relief as she started up the trail again. She was going to be just fine. A short walk through the loop. Richardson had told her it was only a few kilometers, and she could walk that far. Then she could stop somewhere in Calgary for a couple of bottles of water and something to eat, and she'd be back at the office again.

CHAPTER ELEVEN

*M*argie was dragging her feet, but she started to recognize some of the landmarks that showed she was at or near the murder scene. She couldn't remember enough to locate it precisely. It was a lot steeper than she remembered. She wandered off of the path, looking down at the ground for some sign of where Smith's body had been. The vegetation should be crushed—if not by his body, then by the various law enforcement officers and techs gathering forensic evidence and the vehicles that had been parked nearby. There would be some sign that they had been there.

Margie walked back to the trail, went a little farther, and veered off again. It felt closer. But she still wasn't sure.

As she looked around for some sign of where the vehicles had been parked and the yellow tape tied, she suddenly felt as if she were being watched. She stopped and listened. There was no sound of anything but the birds singing and the wind in the trees.

A twig snapped off in the distance somewhere.

An animal? Someone watching her? Someone exploring on their own?

Was someone else looking for the murder scene? Maybe the

killer realized he had dropped something? Or was there a treasure he had been afraid David Smith was going to discover first?

She looked around, trying to pick out a figure in the trees. She couldn't see anyone, but couldn't shake the feeling that she was not alone. Why had Smith been killed there? Was there any significance to the place? Or was it just by chance? A random stranger? As much as she had emphasized to Cathy Lin that most murderers were not random crazies, there were a few. Every now and then, it did happen.

Another twig snapped, from a different direction this time. Margie turned slowly, aware of her peripheral vision, paying attention to whether someone was trailing or flanking her, trying to avoid being seen.

"Excuse me! You're supposed to stay on the pathways!"

The loud male voice made her jump, and Margie whirled around to confront the speaker. For a split-second, she was afraid. The man was closer than she had expected. Big, well-built, not someone whom she was going to be able to beat easily in a physical confrontation, if it came to that. But within a couple of seconds, she recognized him as the RCMP officer who was involved in the investigation.

"Constable Shack."

"Detective Pat." He rolled his eyes and blew out his breath. "It's you. I'm sorry, I didn't recognize you when your back was to me. Figured you were some curiosity-seeker, or maybe our doer, returned to the scene of the crime."

Margie wasn't sure whether she should be insulted that he had identified her as a potential suspect. But there was nothing to say that the killer hadn't been a woman. A sharp blade skillfully handled didn't require the upper body strength of a man to be effective. She wondered whether there was anything in her mailbox from the medical examiner's office yet. They should have had the time to do the postmortem—at least the preliminary results.

"You startled me."

"Sorry about that," he apologized again. "Force of habit. And I have a naturally loud voice. My wife is always getting after me for shouting when as far as I know, I was just using a conversational tone."

"Am I in the right place? Is this where he was?"

"Just a little farther up the trail." He pointed the way and then led her on. "Are you looking for anything in particular?"

It was strange that he had been drawn back there too. Was it because they had so little to go on? They had both returned, hoping to find a little something more to make sense of the situation?

"No. I just needed to see it again. Get it firmly in my mind. See if I could connect up anything… anything that might have been motive. I don't like the idea of a killing without a connection to the killer. There had to be some kind of motive. If it wasn't robbery or drugs or something personal like jealousy or rage, then what was it? What made him kill Smith?"

Shack nodded his agreement.

They went a little farther up the trail, and then Smith indicated the area. "Right over here."

They walked through it silently, separating and casting about on their own. Margie was becoming more and more anxious about Shack being there. She had wanted to be there alone. She had wanted to connect with the murder scene somehow, and having him there was blocking her. She felt like she had to watch him and be aware of him the whole time.

Eventually, they both stopped and looked at each other. "Nothing?" Shack asked.

"No. Nothing."

"Me neither."

She looked carefully at his hands and then his face. He had stooped down a couple of times to examine the ground; she had watched him out of the corner of her eye. But he didn't appear to have picked anything up. If he had, then he was skilled at sleight of hand.

Margie took out her phone to record the GPS coordinates. If she came back again, she would be able to find it on her own. And she might search the GPS coordinates on some treasure hunter sites, just to see if anything popped up. It was far from the village or any artifacts as far as she knew, but it would be worth checking out, just to be sure.

"Calling someone?" Shack inquired.

"No. Just making a note."

He waited, she thought, for an explanation, but she didn't give him anything more. Their departments were cooperating, but that didn't mean that she needed to float all of her ideas past him. They would share evidence and information that had been verified, but she didn't have to tell him everything she was thinking.

She remembered the medical examiner. "Do we have the post results yet?" she asked Shack. "I have been busy with other things and haven't seen it."

"Yeah, about an hour ago. Nothing unexpected. No drugs or poison or tattoos of secret societies." There was a smile in his voice at this joke. Margie didn't smile in return.

"So, nothing of interest."

"Nothing that jumped out at me. But of course, you might see something. I haven't read it in detail yet either, just skimmed through for any red flags."

"Okay. I'll look at it when I get back to the office." Even so, she wanted to make sure that she had received it, so she unlocked her phone and navigated to her mail, running her eye down the list of email subject lines. She tapped to open the email and then the attachment.

One thing she wanted to check just to confirm to herself... she found the description of the stab wound and what the medical examiner had been able to deduce about the blade used and the attacker.

"It was a downward stroke," she pointed out, demonstrating stabbing down into someone.

"Yes," Shack agreed.

"The Fish Creek murder was not. It was lower, and an upward stroke. Someone shorter than the victim. Going up under the ribs instead of trying to stab down through them." Abdul had been trained to kill. He knew a knife went in more easily under the ribs.

"What are the comparative heights of the victims?"

"They were both a shade over six feet."

"And the Fish Creek murder fits with the guy that you arrested. A kid. Someone shorter than him."

"But not this one. For a downward stroke to hit him in the chest where it did at that angle, you're looking for an attacker who is taller than Abdul. Someone closer to six feet tall himself."

"Good to know. But you already checked that it couldn't be the boy anyway, didn't you?"

"Yeah. I just want to eliminate him as a possible suspect in as many ways as possible. He didn't do it. There's no point in speculating that it could have been him."

Shack nodded. "Okay. The kid is off the table. At least there's one thing we know, in a whole lot of nothing."

Margie sighed. "Yeah."

"Can I walk you to your car? You know where it is?"

"Oh, no. I'm fine. I just follow this trail until I get to the parking lot."

He nodded. Margie went back to the pathway and started walking.

"Uh, Detective Pat?"

"What?"

"Other way. Unless you want to take the long way around."

She squinted at the sun, which was too far overhead for her to tell directions by it. She didn't think she was walking back the direction she had come. But she wasn't sure enough to argue with him.

"Oh. Right. Thanks."

She turned around and walked the other direction. She could tell that Shack was watching her all the way until she was out of sight. Even then, she couldn't relax. She couldn't shake the feeling that she was still being watched.

CHAPTER TWELVE

*B*y the time she reached the parking lot, she was exhausted, hungry, thirsty, needed to use the washroom, and was irritated with herself and everyone else for the long hike. It was supposed to be an easy walk. Just a quick zip around the loop. It had ended up being a lot more than that, and she was still jumping out of her skin every time she heard a voice, a dog bark, or a twig snap.

Luckily, there was a washroom just off the parking lot. Only an outhouse, as Ian had told her, but it was better than nothing. That took care of one problem. She then climbed into her car, turned it on, and blasted the air conditioning. She didn't have any water in the car. Maybe she should keep it stocked if she were going to go on unplanned walks in the park.

She pulled back onto Glenbow Road and pointed her car uphill to get back to the highway. She hit her Bluetooth button and called the office. Detective Jones picked up on the third or fourth ring.

"Well, hello, stranger. Long time no see."

"Sorry I've been MIA today. I spent longer at the park than I expected to."

"I hope that means it was a productive trip and you found something."

"No, it was pretty much a bust."

"Pretty much?"

"I ran into Constable Shack out there."

"Really?" Jones's voice was curious. "What was he doing there? You're the primary. I would think that he would let you know if he was chasing anything down."

"Me too. I don't know that he had anything, though. I guess he was just doing the same thing as I was, looking for some clue as to why the killer attacked Smith. There had to be a motive for killing him."

"But you didn't find anything."

"No. Neither of us found anything. Or if he found anything, he didn't tell me about it."

"But you were there together, so he couldn't have found anything."

"I don't think so. It kind of creeped me out, Shack being there at the same time as I was. He had no way of knowing that I would be there. I didn't even know that I was going to be there at just that time."

"So, he wasn't there to meet you."

"No."

"It was just luck that you both ended up there at the same time."

"Exactly." Margie pondered on it. "I felt like I was being watched. Both before I ran into him and after."

"And you think..." Jones trailed off, waiting for Margie to jump in and complete the thought.

"I don't know. Was he watching me? Following me? He offered to walk me to my car. Why? Did he want to make sure that I was really leaving? Or was he being polite? Or did he think that I could be in danger?"

"He's an RCMP constable. I'm sure he was just being polite," Jones said firmly.

Margie wished she could believe it, but her imagination was running overtime. She hated the wired, anxious feeling. She looked in her rear-view mirror. There was a car behind her, but she couldn't see the face of the occupant through the glare on the windshield.

"I saw that the postmortem results came in. I'll have a look at them when I get back. Was there anything else?"

"Nothing that seemed to lead anywhere. An inventory of the items collected at the scene. What has been processed for prints. Pictures. It's kind of weird—"

Suddenly, Jones was gone.

CHAPTER THIRTEEN

*M*argie looked at her display and saw that the call had dropped. She looked in her mirror again at the car that was following her, as if it might somehow be his fault.

What did she think? That he was jamming her signal to keep her from talking to her office? That it was Shack, making sure that she couldn't get some vital piece of information on a piece of evidence that had been processed?

She pulled quickly onto the highway, spraying gravel behind her as if Shack were pursuing her, and she had to get away before he could ram her or force her off the road. The car behind her didn't pull out at such a reckless pace, but smoothly pulled into traffic and hung a few cars back from her. She watched to see if it would stay behind her. It did. But more than likely, he was going back to Calgary just as she was. There was only one way to go to get there. He stayed behind her because she had pulled out quickly and was staying just over the speed limit. He wouldn't pass her unless he broke the speed limit.

She kept an eye on the car, but started to relax. Shack or Dr. Kahn had told her there was a spot where the cell signal dropped, right at the top of the hill where she had been cut off from Jones. That was all it was. Right where you expected the signal to be the best, there was a blind spot and the call would drop. And he had been right.

Feeling silly about her panic, Margie called Jones back. "Sorry, I lost you there. Bad cell signal. What were you saying?"

She still kept an eye out for the car that had followed her off of the park, but tried to push away the anxiety.

"Just that I was hoping you would go through the items that he had on him. Something doesn't feel right."

"What?"

"I don't know. I can't put my finger on it. There's that woman's name and number...?"

"Right, I remember that. Nothing weird about someone writing down a phone number."

"Except today, who writes it on a piece of paper and puts it in his wallet. You'd put it in your phone, wouldn't you?"

"Well, I would, but some people are not big on technology. My mother wouldn't."

"And it's not a phone number."

Margie frowned. "It isn't?"

"Not unless he wrote it down wrong. It's only six digits. I think it is something else. Like a serial number."

Even though Canada had required ten-digit numbers for several years, Margie still often only wrote down the seven digits after the area code, unless it was a different area code from what she expected. Calgary had long been area code 403, and people still left it off when giving their phone numbers or writing them down. Margie hadn't even noticed that the number on the slip of paper was only six digits long.

"Hmm. I guess it could be something else. Maybe... he reported a theft?" Her mood lifted a little. Maybe it was a break in the case. "Maybe... if there was a theft, could it have been related to his murder?"

"I don't know," Jones's tone was doubtful. "That doesn't really... make much sense. How would a serial number lead the police to a burglar? How would killing Smith keep them from finding out?"

"Maybe he hadn't made the report yet, but he was going to. Maybe the killer knew, and he knew that if the report was made, it would lead him to a pawnshop claim ticket or a Kijiji ad. Maybe…?"

"Maybe. But it doesn't feel right."

"Okay. Well, I'll look at it when I get there. Maybe something will come to me. I'm a little muddled right now."

"You'll be here in half an hour or so?"

"Bit longer. I'm going to grab a bite to eat. I haven't had anything today, and I've been walking forever."

"I thought you were going on one of those golf carts?"

"I did for the first part, but then I wanted to walk the Tiger Lily Loop, and I ended up in Badger Bowl…"

Jones giggled. "Are those really the trail names? I like Badger Bowl."

"Yeah, those are really their names. I didn't see any badgers, though."

"Luckily. I understand they're pretty vicious."

"Are you going into Cochrane to eat?"

"Into Cochrane? Why would I? That's the opposite direction."

Margie automatically checked the road sign coming up to confirm that she was driving toward Calgary, not Cochrane.

"Ice cream."

"Ice cream?"

"Yeah, MacKay's. They are the best place in the region to go for ice cream. You have to go there."

"Well… not today. What makes them so good?"

"They make all kinds of cool flavors. They're an institution. They've been there since I was a kid. Since my parents were kids."

"I'll have to take Christina there one day. Make it a mother-daughter date."

"Yeah, you have to do it," Jones said, sounding envious. "I should have told you before you went out there today. I forget that you're not from around here, so you wouldn't know about MacKay's."

Her blood sugar back on an even keel and one bottle of water under her belt, Margie was feeling a lot better when she got back to the squad room. She laughed at herself for being so paranoid about somebody following her or being anxious with Shack being there at the same time as she was. She should be happy to know that he was investigating as well. She needed all of the help she could get.

She said hello to the various team members who were working away busily on their cases, staring at computers, talking on the phone, and making notes on the files. Jones greeted her cheerily. Margie sat down at her computer to look at the evidence again. Everything that had been in Smith's pockets had seemed normal at the time, but she might have overlooked something. Like the woman's phone number not being a phone number.

She brought up the photograph of the piece of paper and studied it.

Stella.

Like her dog. It was always funny to run into familiar names in other places. She didn't think she had ever met a person named Stella. That didn't mean that there weren't any, just that it wasn't a very common name anymore. People associated it with that scene in *A Streetcar Named Desire.* If she went by Jones's instinct that it might be a serial number, then Stella might be a brand name. Margie did a quick internet search.

A fashion company. A new Calgary condo development. Lager. She followed a link to the Stella condos and clicked through a few pages. Maybe Smith had been planning to move. The number could be a real estate listing. A phone number that he'd copied down wrong. Maybe some kind of land titles reference number. She would call around and see if she could find out.

While she was at it, she figured it was time to look at the other items that had been on the body again. Pictures of his phone had been posted, but none of the content. Maybe they hadn't gotten to it yet, or maybe there was nothing on it. Or they were still trying to get it unlocked. Those things could take time. There was a photo that had been in his wallet. His cards.

Margie cracked open her second bottle of water as she leaned forward to study the screen. She had a headache at the back of her head that she thought was from dehydration or the sun, so she needed to drink more. She enlarged the photo on the screen.

Having met Cathy Lin, she expected to find the young woman in the picture somewhere, but she was not there as far as Margie could see. She was too old to be a high school student, if that's what the building in the picture was, but she could be a teacher. She didn't remember asking Lin what her profession was. The picture didn't seem to focus on anyone in particular. Like it was a stock photo of a school, very generic. A day in the life. Apparently, nothing to be found there.

Cards in the wallet. Driver's license, credit cards, bank card, Canoe Club, Calgary Co-op membership, Community Natural Foods membership, Optimum points, library membership. Just a regular guy doing normal, everyday things. No firearms permit. No radical or religious groups. No cards in names other than that of David Smith.

She rubbed the back of her head and neck, hoping the pain and fatigue would go away. She had another sip of water and went back to the workspace for the case to check for further information.

CHAPTER FOURTEEN

*M*argie made sure to get off of work in good time. She could do some more work on the case later in the evening while Christina was working on her homework. But she didn't want Christina to be alone in the house after she got home from school. It was important to make sure she was safe.

Margie wasn't sure what to tell her about the rabbit and her suspicion that someone might be stalking or trying to scare her. Christina knew, of course, that since Margie was a police officer, she could be hurt in the line of duty. They both knew there were risks, though Margie wasn't sure whether Christina understood them as well as someone older and more experienced. Teenagers tended to have a strange relationship with mortality, not understanding how frail human life was and that they and those around them were only on the earth temporarily. They took risks. They acted as if they didn't know the consequences of the things they chose to do. Or as if the rules wouldn't apply to them.

So she didn't know whether Christina would take the news of a stalker in stride, or whether she would overreact to it, or if she would have another reaction that Margie hadn't even foreseen. She had come to accept that Christina was different from her. A separate and independent person with her own headspace. It was sometimes difficult as a parent to understand that this person who had come from her didn't think and react the same way as she did.

So she didn't say anything to start with. She would see if Christina brought it up herself. Then play it by ear.

"Shall we take Stella out for her walk?" Margie asked.

Christina had barely gotten home and might well complain that she needed some time to relax before having to go out again. But instead, Christina seemed relieved by the suggestion. "Yeah. Let's go out. Walkies, Stella!"

Stella went excitedly to the peg her leash hung on and panted happily as she waited for one of them to hook her up. "I think she's ready," Christina laughed.

"Sure looks like it. She's such a good girl!"

Stella's tail swept back and forth, appreciating the praise. Christina attached her lead and they left the house, headed for the pathway along Twenty-Sixth Street. They had to stop every couple of minutes for Stella to sniff at lamp posts and rocks and bugs crawling across the sidewalk and whatever scent signatures the other dogs in the neighborhood had left in the grass and on the trunks of trees. But it was relaxing. A nice, unhurried journey.

"How was school today?"

"It was okay." Christina's shoulders lifted and fell.

"Has it been as bad as you thought it would be?"

Margie knew what answer she wanted to hear. She wanted Christina to tell her that it was fine, that she was adjusting quickly and making friends, and it wasn't as bad as it had seemed the first day when she'd practically had a meltdown over having to go to a new school.

Christina didn't answer at first. They walked along, letting Stella set the pace, breathing the cooling air scented with car exhaust fumes, freshly-cut grass, and a hearty garlic scent from someone's supper cooking in a house they walked past.

"It's been better and worse," Christina said finally.

Margie didn't press for more details, just waited.

"The classes aren't bad, and I think the teachers are ten times better. A lot of stuff is the same wherever you go. Riding on the bus sucks, especially in the middle of a pandemic. School lunches." She rolled her eyes and shook her head. Margie wasn't sure whether she disliked taking lunch to school or buying lunch at the school cafeteria. She had a choice. Maybe she disliked both equally.

"And what's worse?" she prompted eventually, when it seemed that Christina wasn't going to explain any further.

"I didn't think it would be so hard to make friends. I didn't realize how few Métis there would be. And we had lots of racism in Manitoba, but at least there were a lot of us, so we could band together and just shrug it off. But here, it's more subtle, and I don't know who will have my back. There are kids who are not white but have white friends, and there are groups that will only hang out with other kids who are the same race. And there are others that... I just don't know. I'm kind of afraid to get to know the white kids, especially if they're popular, but I know they're not all bad." She shrugged. "I hate being in the youngest grade at the school. It's good because everyone is making new friends with kids who went to different schools than they did, but I don't like being... so vulnerable." Christina sighed and shook her head. "I just wish I didn't have to be there."

"Do you want me to look at other schools? Or do you want to do online? A lot of kids are right now because of the pandemic. No one would think you were weird."

"No," Christina used that long-suffering teenage voice that asked her why Margie was so intent on ruining her life. "I don't want to do that."

"Is there anything I can do?"

"We could go back to Winnipeg." After she said it, she looked at Margie. "I know we can't. You've got a job here..."

"Would you really want to? Go back to the way things were before? Leave Moushoom here by himself?"

Christina scowled, staring down at the pathway as they walked. "I don't know."

"I thought we should bring him out here one day. Do you think he would like that?"

Christina brightened, as she always did when they were talking about her grandfather. "He would like that," she agreed. "But could he? I don't think he can walk very far."

"We could use a wheelchair."

"I think that would be great. He's always so sad, stuck inside like that. He should be out where he can commune with Mother Earth."

"Good. We'll do it, then. Maybe this weekend."

Christina nodded, smiling at the opportunity to do something for Moushoom. They got to the block where they usually turned off to go home. Christina pointed farther down the pathway, where there was a branch off to a steep downhill road.

"What's over there?"

Margie looked for a moment, knowing she had been down that far before when she checked out the route to the bicycle overpass and downtown.

"Oh. The Canoe Club. They put their canoes into the irrigation canal down there."

Christina nodded. "We should try that sometime. Do they do lessons?"

"I don't know. We could find out."

Christina knew that Margie didn't like watersports, so Margie didn't see the need to point it out. If Christina wanted to take some canoe lessons, Margie was sure it could be arranged. She would just be watching with her feet firmly planted on the bank. She was willing to spring for anything that would help Christina to feel like she belonged there.

Or almost anything.

§

SOMETHING HAD BEEN NIGGLING at the back of Margie's mind since she had returned from her walk with Stella and Christina.

She felt uncomfortable and anxious without knowing why. She kept an eye on the windows as it started to get darker, not liking it that she couldn't see out. She turned on the outside lights so that she would know if someone were in the yard again. Christina was doing her homework at the kitchen table with her headphones on, and if she thought this was strange behavior, she didn't bother to say anything about it. Margie wondered how much money it would take to get a good alarm system installed. Or maybe just motion-detecting lights and a webcam, so that they could get a picture of whoever entered the yard.

She sat down at her computer to review the postmortem report on David Smith. She was finding it difficult to focus, but the report didn't say anything she didn't already know. She looked again at the various personal items that they had recovered. Still no more information on the contents of his phone.

Stella

Membership to the Canoe Club

A picture of a high school

Margie sucked in her breath so suddenly that it made her cough and choke. Christina pulled one of the earbuds away from her ear, looking at her. "Are you okay?"

"No!"

Christina looked startled. She got up quickly and went to the sink to run a glass of water for Margie. Margie took it with shaky hands. She took a few sips, trying to calm the racking coughs.

"What happened?" Christina asked. She patted Margie on the back. "Are you choking?"

Margie shook her head and put her hand over her mouth to try to stifle the cough. With her other hand, she pointed at her screen. Stella and a reference number. Christina peered at it and shook her head.

"Stella's license number? What about it?"

Tears running down her face, Margie patted her leg to call Stella to her. She looked at the number on the tag attached to Stella's collar. Christina was right. It was Stella's license number. She forced more of the water down.

"The Canoe Club," she choked out.

"The Canoe Club? Yeah? What about it? Mom, you're being weird. It's like we're playing charades, but I don't even know what the theme is."

Margie scratched Stella's ears and bent down to kiss her on the top of the head, trying to calm the coughing.

"Make sure—the doors—locked."

Christina didn't ask why this time. She just took a few steps to the front door, made sure that the bolt was turned, and then jogged through the kitchen to the back door and checked that one.

"They're locked," she reported back. "Now tell me. What's going on?"

"I just think… something is wrong. I have to call Constable Evans. And Sergeant MacDonald. I think…" Margie cut herself off and shook her head. She couldn't finish the thought. It was like saying what she was thinking was the last line to complete a spell, and if she said it out loud, he might materialize in front of her.

When Constable Evans had come to take her report on the dead rabbit, she had put his business card in her pocket and had not yet entered it into her phone. Margie felt her pockets and eventually came up with the card.

She cleared her throat a few times and seemed to be able to talk without more coughing, though her voice was weak and rough. She grasped Christina's hand before placing the call.

"It's going to be okay, Christina."

"What's okay? I'm scared, Mom."

"I know." Margie looked at the windows again. She still couldn't see anyone outside. Once it was dark, people didn't walk around the neighborhood anymore. Not much. They might drive to the grocery store or to do what other errands they needed to, but they wouldn't be out taking a stroll. There wouldn't be any reason for anyone to be walking down her back alley or peeking into the yard.

She tapped Evans's digits into her phone and waited for it to connect. Of course, she probably wouldn't be able to get him until the next day, when he was back on shift again. If he was even on shift. He might have the day off.

"Evans."

"I'm sorry to be calling you after hours, Constable," Margie apologized. "It's Margie Patenaude, from this morning. The rabbit."

"Yes, I remember you. I'm afraid I don't have anything back on the case yet. These things take a few days. But rest assured, we are taking it seriously."

"There's more. I'm worried... he may be dangerous."

"Has he been back? Do you know who it is?"

"I don't think so. And I'm not sure exactly, but... he may be connected to another case I'm working."

Evans knew that Margie was in Homicide. Christina did too, but she didn't seem to put it together, at least not as quickly as Evans did.

"Oh. I see." His voice was serious. "We'll put a rush on it, then. Are you in danger? You should have called 9-1-1 if it is an emergency."

"I haven't seen him, though, so I don't know that it is. I just... do you think you could send a couple of patrols by tonight? Just to be sure everything is okay?"

"Yes. I'll get on that. Do you have any evidence that ties the two cases together?"

"Can you tell me... how someone would get my dog's license number?"

Evans was silent for a moment. When he spoke, it was in a tone that suggested that Margie might be completely off her rocker. "How would someone get your dog's license number? From you, I guess. Or if they were right there to look at the number on her tag. Or maybe someone who worked in the licensing department."

"Somebody had it."

"Who?"

"Somebody had her name and the license number written down."

"Who?" Evans repeated urgently.

"The Glenbow Park victim. It was in his wallet."

"Oh." He was taken aback, but also calmer upon hearing this. "Well then... if he's dead, he isn't going to do you any harm."

"He was dead before the rabbit. He died... between the squirrel and the rabbit."

"That doesn't make much sense."

"It does... if the killer put it in his wallet."

CHAPTER FIFTEEN

$\mathcal{M}$om... I'm freaking out," Christina said. "I don't get what you're saying here. What do you mean the killer put Stella's number in the dead guy's wallet? Why would he do that?"

"To taunt me." Margie tapped Sergeant MacDonald's number into her phone. "He copied everything he could from the Fish Creek murder so that I would be called in on the Glenbow Park murder too. And then he planted things on the body to taunt me. To tell me that he was close to me, and I didn't even see him there."

She swallowed and held tightly to Christina's hand. Christina squeezed back. Neither let go.

Margie's phone was in speaker mode so that she didn't have to pick it up and could continue to hold Christina's hand and to work her mouse at the same time.

"Patenaude?" MacDonald said sharply.

"Sir. I'm sorry to call you at home. I may have a break on the case. And... I might need some help."

"Of course. What have you got?"

"You remember the name Stella and the number on the paper in his wallet?"

"Yes."

"That's the name and license number of my dog."

She gave him a moment to process that. It didn't take him long.

"He knows you."

"He must. He couldn't get that number from anywhere else. Unless he works in the licensing department. He could only get it from me or by looking at Stella's collar tags. And I didn't give it to anyone. He wanted me to know... that he's been close to me."

"It's an assumption, but let's go with it. Was there anything else on Smith's body that was suspicious?"

"His address is close to Glenbow."

"Yes. Makes sense, that's why he's able to walk there frequently."

"But he had a membership card for the Canoe Club."

"They must canoe on the Bow over there. Put out on the water in Cochrane, maybe."

"Do you know where the Canoe Club is?"

"No."

"It's two blocks from my house."

"And you're not in the northwest."

"I'm about as far from there as you can get."

"You're in Forest Lawn, aren't you?"

"Almost. Greater Forest Lawn."

"It still might make sense. He could be a member of the Canoe Club and still canoe over by the park. It's a possibility."

"Yes."

"Anything else?"

Margie gave Christina's hand a tug, encouraging her to sit down on the couch beside her. Christina sat down and put her arm around Margie.

"Sir, you're on speaker and my daughter is here." She probably should have told him that at the beginning of the conversation.

"Christina, right? How are you, Christina? Hanging in there?"

"Yes," Christina said in a small voice.

Margie clicked through images on her computer. "Christina. Can you look at this picture?"

Christina leaned in toward the screen. She nodded.

"Where is this picture taken? Do you know?" Margie asked.

"Yeah. That's my school. Forest Lawn High."

"Are you sure?"

"Yes."

"Sir, that picture found on Smith—" Margie started to tell MacDonald.

Christina put her finger directly onto Margie's computer screen. "You see… there I am. Right there."

Margie wouldn't have recognized the back view of her daughter. The sliver of her caught in the photograph was too small. But she realized that the shirt and pants could have been Christina's, and the girl in the picture had long black hair. Margie took another swallow of her water, trying to wash down the lump that was suddenly stuck in her throat.

"Christina, are you saying you're in the picture that was found at the homicide scene?" MacDonald demanded.

"If that's where this picture is from. Yes."

"It is," Margie agreed.

"I don't like this," MacDonald said. "I want someone there with you. Especially considering—the other thing we discussed this morning."

"Christina knows about the squirrel and the rabbit," Margie told him. "And I already called Constable Evans to ask him if they would send patrols by the house."

"This guy clearly knows a lot about you, including where you live and where Christina goes to school. He's planted clues to let you know he's out there watching. You don't know who he is?"

Margie drew in a long breath and let it out slowly, trying to clear her mind. Who had been close enough to them to see Stella's dog tags? Had he been in the yard? Maybe Stella had run up to greet him when he had planted the squirrel. She was a gentle creature and would have considered a stranger who brought her a dead squirrel her new best friend.

Had he been following them? Or was it someone they knew?

"We don't have the parking lot video yet?" Margie asked.

"Not yet. I'll light a fire under someone. And I don't know if the phone will hold any clues… it is possible that he took a picture of the view and managed to catch the killer in the frame at some point. I doubt we would be so lucky, but I'll push to get that phone cracked too. I'd like someone there with you tonight, just in case… Do you have any preferences?"

"Well… two single gals here… I'd rather it was a woman, so we don't have to be worried about walking around in our PJ's."

"Jones, then?"

"Yes."

"I'll see if she's available. If I can't get her, you'll take someone else on the team?"

"Yes. Of course."

"Okay. Expect one of the team on your doorstep within a couple of hours. Don't open the door without verifying who it is first."

"I won't."

He hung up the call without saying goodbye. Christina leaned her head down onto Margie's shoulder and stayed cuddled there, like she was a little girl again, and not a couple of inches taller than Margie.

"Are you okay?" Margie asked.

"Yes."

"It's scary."

"Yeah."

"But you're okay?"

"I'm here with you."

"Is it all right with you if I get my gun out?"

Christina nodded.

While Margie's duty weapon stayed in her locker at work when she returned home at the end of the day, she did have a personal weapon at home. She left Christina sitting on the couch and went to her bedroom closet, retrieving the gun and ammunition from the gun safe on the shelf. She had never needed it for personal protection before. She kept it oiled and took it to the range every couple of months, but she had never before felt like she needed it. She returned to her seat beside Christina and lay the gun down within reach on the side table.

Christina didn't return to her homework, cuddling up to Margie once more. Margie turned on the TV to provide a distraction. Neither of them paid it as much attention as they normally would have, aware of every noise that Stella or the house made as they sat there waiting for something to happen.

CHAPTER SIXTEEN

*M*orning came too soon for Margie. She hadn't slept more than a couple of hours, and what little sleep she'd gotten had been restless and plagued by nightmares. She peeked in on Christina and found that she was still asleep. Detective Jones was still sitting in the living room, prowling occasionally to each of the windows to check for any intruders.

"Hi," Margie greeted softly. "No trouble?"

"No. Quiet neighborhood. Some neighbors heading out to work already, a few walkers, but nothing suspicious."

Stella whined at Margie and took a few steps toward the door, wanting to be let out. Margie ducked into Christina's room to look out the window. It was still dark but, with the outside lights on, the yard was fairly well illuminated, and she couldn't see anything suspicious.

"I'm just going to check out the yard before I let Stella out," she told Jones. "Make sure we don't have any more little surprises."

"Take your gun with you."

Margie wanted to argue that it wasn't necessary, but she didn't. She retrieved her weapon and went outside, preventing Stella from following her out until she could clear the yard. Stella barked and yipped in protest.

Margie took a quick turn around the yard, but didn't find any dead animals this time. She heard footsteps crunching down the alley and followed them with her eyes, waiting for the walker to come into view. She relaxed when she saw it was Oscar. He smiled and waved at her

"Hello, Oscar. Hi, Milo." She couldn't see Milo walking beside him, but could hear him panting and his chain jingling.

"Looks like it's going to be a nice day," Oscar observed. Margie agreed. He kept walking, disappearing from her view a few houses down. Margie went back to the door and let Stella out. She stood in the doorway with Jones, watching Stella race around the yard and then check out each of her scent posts one at a time.

"That was one of your neighbors?" Jones asked.

"Yes. And no."

Jones raised her brows in query.

"I know him from walking the dogs. He walks Milo and we walk Stella. We run into each other on the pathway. Stop and talk for a minute sometimes."

They were both silent.

"He's a nice guy," Margie said.

"Nothing suspicious there, then?"

"No."

Margie gave Stella a couple more minutes and then called her back in. She got herself a cup of coffee. Christina came out of her room, blinking owlishly.

"Hi," Margie greeted, and pulled Christina close to kiss her on the forehead. "How are you this morning?"

"I didn't think he lived over here," Christina said, and it was an instant before Margie connected that Christina was talking about Oscar. She must have heard her talking with Jones or seen her wave at Oscar. "I thought he was in Dover. Just... not here. I've never seen him in the neighborhood before. Only on the pathway."

Margie nodded.

She looked at Jones, who was standing nearby listening. "She's right."

CHAPTER SEVENTEEN

*M*argie was reluctant to let Christina get on the bus to go to school. Christina told her with forced cheerfulness that everything would be fine and gave her a hug and a kiss on the cheek, then ran to catch the bus just in time. Margie watched until the bus was out of sight. There didn't appear to be anyone following it, friend or stranger.

In a few minutes, Margie was on her way back to Glenbow Park. It would take her nearly an hour. She couldn't help being nervous about what the day would bring. She tried deep breathing when she got out to the ring road. She tried chanting. She tried putting her de-stress music list on the radio.

None of it helped very much. Margie was still just as anxious when she got to the Glenbow Road turnoff from the highway. She looked behind her as she slowed down to make the turn, but couldn't see anyone tailing her.

The Alberta Parks guy that MacDonald had talked to told her the gate would be unlocked for her; she just had to get out of her car to swing it open. Then she could drive down to the Park Office. There she would meet with someone who would have the various surveillance videos for her.

She had known that the gate would be a pinch point. She

could feel eyes on her as she got out of her car to open it. She brushed her fingers over her gun in its holster. As she walked to the gate, another car drove down Glenbow Road and pulled to the side. A tall figure got out. Margie watched with a sense of disbelief as his dog jumped out to join him. Man and his dog. Doing everything together.

"Margie!" Oscar smiled pleasantly. "Fancy running into you here! I thought you would be at work by now."

It was, of course, no coincidence that he was there. Despite Margie not being able to see him behind her on the way over, one of the tail cars had picked him up and informed Margie of the fact.

"You're very smart, aren't you?" she asked Oscar blandly. "You had everyone fooled."

His eyes narrowed a little. "I don't know about that," he said. "The news never reported any connection between the two murders."

"No one ever thought they were the same killer. They were just similar enough to get me over here to investigate."

He nodded. "That was all I wanted."

She could tell that he was bursting with pride. Excited to tell her how smart he had been. How he had planted every clue and watched her trying to break the case, laughing at her when they would meet on their evening walks.

She could see him in her mind, making a fuss over Stella, scratching her ears and telling her what a good dog she was. Cuddling her close to his face. Close enough to see her license number.

"You took longer than I thought to figure out the clues. I thought you would get *Stella* right away."

"And when I figured that out, was I supposed to know that it was you?"

"No." He laughed. "I could tell you were suspicious this morning. But that didn't stop you from coming back here. Why did you need to come back here again when you were here so long yesterday?"

So he *had* been watching her. It hadn't just been an overactive imagination.

Oscar was walking toward her. Just inching forward every now and then, like if he did it slowly enough she wouldn't know he was within striking distance until it was too late. It was difficult for Margie not to pull her gun immediately to protect herself.

"I came for the surveillance tapes. To see if I could find you on any of them."

He nodded. "Well, you're not going to get the chance, I'm afraid."

His hand was in his pocket. Holding an open knife, if she weren't mistaken.

"Why would you do all of this? Go to all this risk? Kill a man you didn't even know just to get my attention?" Her voice was getting higher and louder, though she tried to keep it under control.

"*Detective* Patenaude," he said slowly, sounding each syllable out distinctly. "You didn't tell me you were a cop when we first met. Or any time after that."

"It didn't come up. We just talked about the dogs and the weather."

"You thought you were smarter than me, but you weren't."

He took another step toward her, closing in quickly, pulling his hand with the knife in it out of his pocket and raising it to stab downward into her chest, as he had with David Smith. But Margie had her gun clear of the holster, and there were shouts from half a dozen other police officers who had been watching and listening from their vantage points, now visible with guns raised and shouting at him to freeze.

Oscar looked around at them, stunned. "How...?" He dropped his knife and raised his hands, giving them no reason to shoot him. He blinked, baffled.

Margie secured him in handcuffs and patted him down before

answering. "It was a good idea you had, using Stella's license number."

He shook his head. "What?"

"I didn't know your last name or where you lived. So we looked up Milo. There aren't very many dogs named Milo licensed in the southeast. Actually, just one in the Greater Forest Lawn area."

"But you didn't know I was coming here! You didn't know I was following you again."

"I didn't see you. You're pretty good. But the cars a kilometer back were able to spot your vehicle, when they knew what to look for. And *I* knew where I was going, even if you didn't. So that officers closer to the scene could get here ahead of us."

His usual wide, white smile was gone. His face was red with fury. She waited for him to shout at her that it was not fair, that she had cheated. And maybe she had. She hadn't let him play out the game the way he had wanted to.

But he said nothing more.

CHAPTER EIGHTEEN

I don't get it." Margie sighed as she worked her way through the reports that had to be filed to document all the evidence that had pointed to Oscar as a suspect, and his capture and arrest in the park. "What would make a person do something like this? So random and... so bizarre. He didn't even know Smith. He did it all just so he could feed me clues and watch me work the case?"

Detective Cruz was leaning against Detective Jones's desk nearby, giving her a hand in getting everything filled out properly and offering his own commentary on the case.

"Not much in his background that explains it. No prior arrests. No restraining orders. He seems to be a law-abiding citizen, right down to properly licensing his dog."

"And picking up after him," Margie contributed. "He was always very diligent. Never 'forgot' his bags at home or pretended not to notice a mess."

"I did find one thing," Jones offered, catching a stray curl of blond hair and smoothing it away as she stared at her computer screen.

Margie waited for more information. Cruz leaned toward Jones to look at her computer screen. "What?"

"He washed out of the police academy."

Margie stopped typing. Other keyboards and discussions all went silent at the same time. The room was still, everybody listening in.

"He was a cop?" Margie demanded, flabbergasted.

"He wanted to be. Did fine at the written test and initial screening." Jones's fingers tapped the keys lightly, the key-clicks loud in the silent bullpen. "But during training... something happened. He dropped out. Resigned or was asked to leave; there aren't really any details here. You would have to talk to his trainer." A few clicks of the mouse to drill deeper for the information. "Christensen." Jones paused. "Elizabeth Christensen."

Margie's mind went back to Oscar's words. *You didn't tell me you were a cop.... You thought you were smarter than me.* The anger in his tone. Accusation.

"He had problems training under a woman," she guessed. "Doesn't think we should be cops. Much less to be successful at something. Like at being a homicide detective."

Cruz and Jones were both nodding.

"And not just a woman," Cruz pointed out, "but a Native woman. You've heard, haven't you, about how all these ethnics are pushing out the qualified white men?" His sarcastic tone dispelled any thought that he gave such an attitude any credence.

"You'd better watch out," Margie warned. "They'll be coming after your job next."

"I'm not a white ma—" Cruz caught the glimmer in Margie's eyes and cut himself off. He shook his head, letting out a puff of breath. "You almost had me there, Detective Pat. Almost."

Margie winked at Jones.

It hadn't been *almost* at all.

MARGIE HAD one more trip to make to Glenbow Ranch Provincial Park. It wasn't exactly on her way home, and it was hard for her to take that time away from her family, but she believed that community policing in Calgary meant more than just catching the bad guy and going on to the next file.

Justice and healing required more than an arrest.

After she parked her car in the staff parking area, a woman came out to meet her. Long, brown hair, fine wrinkles around her eyes, and a light step as she approached Margie and offered her hand to shake.

"Alice," she offered, as Margie squeezed her thin, dry hand. "I'm glad to meet you in person, Detective Pat."

"Thank you. You're sure this is okay? I don't want to do anything that would get you in trouble or reflect badly on the police department if someone complained."

"Oh, no," Alice proclaimed. "We acknowledge this is Treaty 7 land. Our First Nations have been allowed to perform ceremonies here. It's never been a problem."

Margie had run into many people who mouthed treaty acknowledgments as they were expected to when they clearly didn't mean or understand them, but Alice seemed to be sincere.

"Even though I'm not part of that treaty?" Margie asked, making sure there could be no misunderstanding.

"Of course not. We know you're Métis. But it isn't like you're some blond-haired thirteen-year-old making excuses for starting a grass fire."

"Okay. Thank you."

Margie had made the decision not to go all the way down to where David Smith had been murdered. She didn't want to get lost or spend that much more time away from her family. She walked instead into a stand of trees a short distance away, the closest wilderness space, and prepared herself.

Despite Alice's words, she watched Margie from a distance, eyes sharp to make sure that there were not any sparks or embers that might start the dry grasses on fire. Margie ignored her. She unfastened her braid that had been coiled into a bun and let it hang down her back.

Margie took several items out of her shoulder bag. She draped the sash that had been given to her by her band before leaving Winnipeg around her shoulders.

She unwrapped the bundle of sacred herbs and placed them in the smudge bowl. She lit them with a match and blew gently to make them smoke. Smudging was not actually a traditional part of Métis culture, but her people were open to new rituals and traditions, and many had adopted smudging as part of their spiritual practice.

Thinking about Smith, she offered the bowl in each of the four directions. The smudge smoke drifted down the hill. Margie started a low chant, praying for healing for Smith's girlfriend and family, for the family who had discovered his body and the other park users who had been troubled by it. For the police and professionals who had all helped to gather the evidence to address the wrong that had been committed.

And for Oscar, a man whose soul had been so hurt that he had struck out in violence against someone he didn't even know, and someone he thought he did.

She prayed for peace and healing for them all.

When the herbs stopped smoking, Margie picked up a hand bell and tolled out nine chimes. The low ringing of the bell stretched out over the landscape and faded like the smoke.

Margie packed her things and left the park without looking back.

CHAPTER NINETEEN

*C*hristina wanted a turn pushing the wheelchair, so Margie let her take over. As the sun started to set, there was a chilly wind setting in. She bent down to tuck the extra blanket around Moushoom to make sure that he was comfortable.

"How is that? Are you nice and toasty?"

"This is wonderful," he said comfortably. "It has been so long since I was able to get out."

Margie smiled, pleased that her idea had been a good one. Moushoom wrapped his hands around his Tim's hot chocolate and raised it to his mouth for a sip. "It is nice to have family around me, and to be able to get out into the fresh air and make contact with nature again."

It wasn't exactly like he was in the wilds. Maybe one day, she would take him to Glenbow Park for a cart tour. Then he could really get out somewhere that he could connect with Mother Earth. But for now, he was happy being out on the pathway, with the long, yellowing grass beside him, trees growing in little bunches putting on their autumn colors, and people out for a stroll or to walk their dogs. Stella waited patiently for them to start walking again, her tongue hanging out of her mouth.

"I'm glad we could all get out together too. I like that we live close and can come by for a visit whenever we want. I'm sorry it's been a few days, I've been tied up with work."

He nodded and had another sip of hot chocolate. "Remind me again what it is that you do."

Others in the extended family had whispered about the possibility of senility, but to Margie, Moushoom had seemed sharp and aware in the times they had seen him so far. This was the first time that he appeared to have forgotten something she had told him. But he couldn't be expected to remember every piece of information, could he?

They started walking again, Margie staying beside Moushoom, where he could still hear and see her.

"I'm a police detective," she reminded him. "I work on the homicide squad."

"Homicide." Moushoom shook his head slowly. "That must be very hard on you."

"Well, it's not easy. But our solve rate is eighty percent. We do good work."

"I didn't mean that it was hard to solve them," he said, as if that should have been obvious. "I mean, it is hard on your mind and your spirit."

"Oh. Yes, I guess so." She didn't know how long it would take her to get over the nightmares or to stop jumping at every little sound in the house, to stop herself from checking on poor Christina every fifteen minutes.

And even though she had known that they needed to take Stella out for a walk and she wanted to take Moushoom out, it had been hard to make herself put her plan into action.

She felt vulnerable walking on the pathway as the sunlight began to fade, and they were left in twilight, and then in darkness. She scrutinized every face as people walked by them, looked at every dog. She knew logically that it had only been one man; only one dog walker had been dangerous. But that didn't stop her brain from checking every single face and dog to make sure that it wasn't Oscar and Milo, or someone else who might have bad feelings toward her.

As safe as the pathway seemed, she wasn't sure she would ever feel one hundred percent safe again.

GLENBOW RANCH PROVINCIAL PARK

In 2006, the children of Alberta rancher Neil Harvie sold 3,246 acres of land to the Government of Alberta to conserve the land, fulfilling the vision of their father. At that time, the author was working as a legal assistant with Andy Crooks, the family's lawyer, and had an insider's view as plans for the park rolled out. She was involved in and present at the park opening in 2011.

Workman has worked closely with the Glenbow Ranch Park Foundation (a non-profit organization that handles many of the visitor services for the park) on a number of levels and like many of the stewards and Calgary west/Cochrane residents, considers it "her park."

As indicated in the title and storyline, the park features some challenging hills. It is a dry park, so when you visit, be sure to bring your water bottle!

Did you enjoy this book? Reviews and recommendations are vital to making a book successful.

Please leave a review at your favorite book store or review site and share it with your friends.

Don't miss the following bonus material:
Sign up for mailing list to get a free ebook
Read a sneak preview chapter
Other books by P.D. Workman
Learn more about the author

Sign up for my mailing list at pdworkman.com
and get Gluten-Free Murder for free!

JOIN MY MAILING LIST AND

Download a sweet
mystery for free

PREVIEW OF DARK WATER
UNDER THE BRIDGE

CHAPTER 1

The sun was still low in the sky, orange light filtering into the kitchen. Margie "Detective Pat" Patenaude was sipping her morning coffee and staring into the depths of her fridge, trying to decide whether to make herself a bag lunch to take to the police station with her, or whether she would take a break and go find something over lunch. She hadn't explored many restaurants near the office, so she wasn't sure what was available. Not that she was that picky.

"The same things are in there as the last time you opened the door," Christina teased, echoing the same words Margie used when her daughter stood staring vacantly into the fridge. "Nothing new is going to materialize while you stand there with the door open."

"You're a smart aleck," Margie told her.

But Christina was right. Margie already knew what was in the fridge, and inspiration wasn't going to strike just because she was standing there with the door open, letting all of the cold air spill to the floor and raising the energy bill. She sighed and closed it.

"I don't know what I want today."

"We need to go shopping. Get something good."

"I think you're right," Margie agreed. They could go to the

Co-op, or the No Frills down Seventeenth Avenue, and stock up on some easy to prepare meals. Margie never seemed to have the time or energy to make much when she got home from work.

The phone rang. Margie looked at it, hoping it would just be some telemarketer so she could ignore it. She didn't want to have to deal with a real phone call so soon. She didn't even have one cup of coffee down yet. But it was Detective Cruz, a Filipino-born cop on her team.

"Patenaude," she answered briskly.

"Is this Detective 'Parks' Pat?" There was a note of amusement in Cruz's voice.

"Parks Pat?" That was a new one. Margie understood where the nickname came from, of course. Since she had moved to Calgary, she had been primary on a murder in Fish Creek Park first, and then a similar one in Glenbow Ranch Provincial Park. They had not been related, except by circumstances, but both had been reported in the news, and it would seem that she had now earned her homicide team nickname. Parks Pat.

"That's what they're calling you," Cruz acknowledged.

"Well, okay. It could be worse. What did you need?"

"Have you ever been to Ralph Klein Park?"

Margie let out a puff of breath. "Ralph Klein Park. No, I haven't even heard about that one. Is it out there near Glenbow?"

"No, actually this one is close to you. That's why I figured you might have been there. It's new. Just opened in 2011."

Margie thought about the little park she had visited while taking Stella out on a walk with Christina. It had a little pond and a splash park for young children. She couldn't remember the name off the top of her head, but was sure it wasn't the one that Cruz was talking about. "Another provincial park?"

"City of Calgary park, this one. Though it might be out of city limits, I'm not clear on that. It's right on the eastern edge of the city, anyway. Think you could get out there?"

"Yes, of course. What... am I going to find there?"

"We've got another body. Sorry."

Well, that was to be expected when she worked homicide. "Another body in another park? But we know it isn't either of the same killers, because we already caught them both. They're locked up where they can't do any more harm. Was it the same cause of death?"

"You'll have to get more information when you get out there, but preliminary indications are that it is not. No visible stab wounds on this one."

"Good. I think if it was the same cause, I might have been a little freaked out."

"We're all a little on edge. I'm going to head out there before long too; I'll back you up."

Margie wondered why he hadn't gone to investigate first. If he was the one who had taken the call. "I'm primary on this one? Why?"

He chuckled. "Because they asked for you in particular."

"Me?"

"Parks Pat. They figured if it's in a park, you should be the one in charge."

"That's just—"

"I know. And don't worry, I'm sure that sooner or later you'll get a body that wasn't found in a park. But for now, that's your assignment. Go to the park, make nice, find out what you can about our newest victim."

❧

Dark Water Under the Bridge is book 3 in the *Parks Pat Mysteries* series and can be ordered at pdworkman.com

ABOUT THE AUTHOR

Award-winning and USA Today bestselling author P.D. (Pamela) Workman writes riveting mystery/suspense and young adult books dealing with mental illness, addiction, abuse, and other real-life issues. For as long as she can remember, the blank page has held an incredible allure and from a very young age she was trying to write her own books.

Workman wrote her first complete novel at the age of twelve and continued to write as a hobby for many years. She started publishing in 2013. She has won several literary awards from Library Services for Youth in Custody for her young adult fiction. She currently has over 60 published titles and can be found at pdworkman.com.

Born and raised in Alberta, Workman has been married for over 25 years and has one son.

𐫗

Please visit P.D. Workman at pdworkman.com to see what else she is working on, to join her mailing list, and to link to her social networks.

𐫗

If you enjoyed this book, please take the time to recommend it to other purchasers with a review or star rating and share it with your friends!

f facebook.com/pdworkmanauthor

twitter.com/pdworkmanauthor

instagram.com/pdworkmanauthor

a amazon.com/author/pdworkman

BB bookbub.com/authors/p-d-workman

g goodreads.com/pdworkman

in linkedin.com/in/pdworkman

p pinterest.com/pdworkmanauthor

youtube.com/pdworkman

CPSIA information can be obtained
at www.ICGtesting.com
Printed in the USA
LVHW031920200821
695769LV00004B/69